TILL WE CAN KEEP AN ANIMAL

Megan Voysey-Braig

The 2007/08 European Union Literary Award was made possible by the generous support of the European Union and the financial support of the French Institute of South Africa, the Goethe-Institut South Africa, the British Council, Embassy of the Kingdom of the Netherlands, the Embassy of Sweden, the Embassy of Spain and the Embassy of Finland.

First published by Jacana Media in 2008

10 Orange Street
Sunnyside
Auckland Park 2092
South Africa
+2711 628 3200
www.jacana.co.za

ISBN 978-1-77009-639-4

The poem on page 138 is an extract from
    TS Eliot's *Preludes* (1917).
Set in Sabon 11/14.6pt
Printed by CTP Book Printers, Cape Town
Job no. 000859

See a complete list of titles at www.jacana.co.za

For my late Grandmother Elizabeth.

My heartfelt thanks to the countries of
The European Union in association with Jacana
Media, for making this book possible.
Thank you to my editors, Maggie Davey
and Natalie Gillman.
To Emily Amos for being there.
To my partner for supporting me throughout.
To my family for believing.
To the Smiths for cheering the loudest.
To Kim for praying.

I find that my heart has been broken by insults.
Hebrew Bible

The world embarrasses me and I cannot dream that
this watch exists and has no watchmaker.
Voltaire

1

IT IS LONELY BEING DEAD. Trust me. I didn't expect it so suddenly, especially on a night like that, a night that was meant to be celebrated. I wasn't young, my death wasn't a tragically untimely ending, the way a child's death is. There is a difference, but I wasn't old. My life ended five years shy of my sixtieth birthday. I still had something to say, I still had some life left to live, I still wanted to experience the rain and the sun on its endless course. I found that life got better the older I became, I was more comfortable in my own skin and less afraid and concerned about what another might think of me. Or even what the world in its wider circle might think of me. Bittersweet: the way you wish you knew the things at twenty that you know at forty. When you really know how to live, your knees give in and your joints ache and senility starts setting in a memory at a time. It takes all that long awkward time to not care anymore about the smaller things or even the bigger things. I often longed to find a way to not feel without being dead; but love always drifted through and over my head and I could never catch its kite tails, which always slipped through my fingers. I simply never understood love. As I never did find my way to being heartless I often thought (who doesn't?) of suicide. Leaning over a balcony that is high enough, holding a pill that is strong enough. But when life is over from your own hand or somebody else's you will give anything to go back. I know this now.

I long to hear the words, long for a dream I keep on dreaming, the same dream in someone's mouth as they breath their last. Who would know about it, what their last breath thought? I want to understand, want to cut a word open and let the air out, be it foul and pestilent, be it fair and sunny weather.

Was this place worth its struggle? Was it not rotten from the beginning? I don't know what to think, being dead because of it. I am a story in a newspaper, the pages in the middle, maybe next to the cartoons. I am a story that is nowhere to be seen, catch me on the flip-side when I come back with my head full of broken glass, my head in my hands to tell you what my last thought was.

I thought I would stop thinking once I was dead; that all pain, all memory, every desire, every injustice and happiness ceases to exist along with all biological functions. Breathing that is beautiful, when you can't draw it in, breathing that was only ever unconscious and involuntary when alive. I dream of air, molecules of oxygen that would reverse the way I look at myself, pale and cold, sewn up in places, and the relatives left behind who don't like to see how the beloved has died. The morticians make it all neat and tidy and unnatural-looking for those left mourning, stricken like children, biting and twisting their lips. Is the way I died an affront to their sensitive constitutions, something that cannot be seen, or is it out of respect for my dead and gone motionless body?

Nobody really wants to see the insides of another, those dark nameless places, globular and bloody, parts that congeal and coalesce, that leak and stink. Slimy primordial parts, however uninformed you are about physiology and branch after branch of enquiry and discovery, a body and its intense fragility compels us to feel nothing more than instant revulsion when it comes apart, when it runs from a wound, when its organs are torn from their moorings. This explains people being sick at crime scenes. That sadistic pseudo sexual pastime of stopping at traffic accident scenes is formed from dreadful fascination. I am not sure how I could have looked any other way, how I could have presented my death in a less nauseating fashion. Even in death we are covered up, made to feel ashamed, cleaned up, scrubbed, disinfected, buried or burnt. Why could no one look at me, why did they turn their heads away and gasp, hold their stomachs? If I could look at myself sitting there in the chair I liked to read in, if I could know that I was not coming back, why could no one comfort me?

Why did no one hold me? Especially my husband. I expected that from him at least. A gesture of tenderness, his index finger stroking my cheek the way he liked to wake me up in the mornings. I know I am being irrational and there was no way he could have known I was still there, just in another state. I was so very afraid, screaming so loudly from an infinitely silent place in that room where he found me. The police were lethargic and apathetic and asked what I assume are the usual questions, as they dusted the counters and the handles for fingerprints. No one looked my way, no one could see what I was seeing and I wasn't sure what had happened to me because I still felt, I could still see everything around me as though I could reach out and touch it, all of it, but my hands went through it. I made no impression at all.

My husband, my lover, secret and warm in the early mornings when I could curl around him, stood frozen and wooden, staring at his feet. I saw the way he began to shake as if some terrible cold place had come to visit him and would never ever leave him.

You are right to fear death, though this country makes excuses and reasons to welcome it all the time, creating situations where death is commonplace; like stepping out for the paper or into the world on the way to work, you never really know if it is your last time, your last round. In your own bed, in your own personal horizon, death is the worst thing that can happen to you when you are not prepared or ready for it, yet the invisible physics that makes this country turn tell you that you have nothing to fear, that the spiral isn't turning and hurtling towards the ground. It will tell you that everything, every possible angle, is being explored to contain it and it is contained. There are no alarm bells ringing here, relax. Don't go looking over your shoulder, don't let your heart throb in your throat down an unlit street, or even in the broadness and clarity of daylight, don't fear your front gate, your door or your home, don't fear the poverty you are in and life that never changes. Everyone can go somewhere, everyone can succeed. This is the rainbow nation, don't forget its primary colors, its possibilities. I am dead and I shouldn't be.

I should tell you now, in case you were wondering, that there is no great white light that fetches you. No chariot is going to swing low and sweet for you and take the misery of dying and leaving the world away from you. Books will tell you differently. The choirs of angels and the gates of heaven, the land of milk and honey, if it is true I haven't seen it yet. Some books even tell you that if you have gone before your time, angels comfort you, making your transition into the next life less traumatic. They will tell you that there are softly lit rooms in another dimension used for this specific transition. Esoteric bunk I read once when I doubted the meaning of existence, doubted the validity of my face in the mirror. I tried to call upon my very own angel, the one that facilitated every move I made in this life. Think of the first name that comes into your head, the text read, and that is your angel. What could be simpler? I tried to drift away into a dreary dream state, thinking that it would help, that a fantastical name would drop into my head like a bright silver coin. All I came up with was dead Uncle Bruce and he was a blatant misogynist and a proud and terrible racist who had a penchant for hunting defenseless game. The brown doe eyes in the sight of his rifle, his fat biltong-greased finger pressed to the trigger. I could hardly watch it, the way it fell, leaving a perfect stillness and emptiness where it had once been.

Yes, Uncle Bruce liked to feel me up on those hunting trips, me pressed up against a thorn tree scorched in the highveld heat; and what transpired was just as strange to me as the buck falling with hardly any sound at all. While Uncle Bruce breathed heavily in my ear, I looked up to the blue sky that didn't seem real to me, angular and hard it was, merciless and unforgiving as vultures scanned the parched ground for dying or already dead animals. And I thought this was a nothing land, made up of men with thick tree stump legs and even thicker necks casting miserable cheerless shadows above all the peripheries my eyes glazed over, where streams retreated and waterfalls went back over the rushing rivers and flowers never opened their faces. I thought, I am a curse forever cast out of love. Uncle Bruce would never think I possessed the mind to think of such things. I was just a stupid child who went to bed when she was told. Still, I sang the dead songs of my innocence as he bucked and shoved between my legs. Afterwards he would peel an orange for me, smile underneath his wide moustache, his bushy eyebrow raised in a wink. My Aunt Hester would have a heavy meal waiting for us when we got home. A dead buck was slung over Uncle Bruce's shoulder, dumped unceremoniously on the porch and his meaty fists shovelling the fork into his mouth, speaking with his mouth full and my guts turned and I don't think they have ever stopped turning, as I stayed sickened to my stomach to the end. I would tell my mother when I finally got home that I didn't like the game farm and the holidays there.

"Sarah," she said, "give your mother a break, I hardly get a moment's rest. I like those holidays with you away." Men made women too tired to love their children, so how could I blame her, stuck as she was with my father.

I refused to believe that he, Uncle Bruce, dead and gone, was looking after my interests and I took the book, the one that promised me angels, to one of those secondhand bookstores I liked to get lost in. Someone else can believe it; for someone else, the names of angels.

So here I am still in the dimension I had lived in for 55 years and these visions, these angelic truths, must have been someone's drug trip for there is no escaping here and no forgetting. *Going before your time*. I doubt the validity of such a statement now. As though it is terribly sad and wasteful to have a life cut short. It doesn't mean anything much in particular. People and animals and every kind of thing that can sense the smallest hum of life leave it all the time in a random disorientated fashion: chaotic and thoughtless. We go when we go and that is all there is to it. Your meaning, your time, stops at any particular point on the watch and you just happen to be there for it. Now that my life has ended I am not sure what to do with the rest of this sense, the rest of these vibrations that keep me conscious and keep me sore.

My time ended at fifteen minutes past seven in the evening, I remember watching the clock on the sensible cream-coloured kitchen wall as I felt myself struggle and claw for breath, but breath would not come. There was nothing but a perfect and complete darkness for what felt like a very long time. It was like being in the deepest part of sleep without the possibility of ever waking up. When I came back I was standing outside, contemplating my broken body. I remember feeling an abject sadness that this had happened and an inconsolable emptiness that no one alive or dead could soothe or comfort.

What was I doing before I was attacked? I can trace it from here, recalling every move, graceful and savage, and every sway and curve towards the end of my life. I had poured myself a drink at the kitchen counter, having just bathed. William and I were going out to celebrate his retirement. I had suggested it, having seen him look so glum the whole week as though he had no reason for existing anymore. I took time, filling the bathroom with steam and potions and restorative elixirs, perfumes. I took care to begin the process of looking beautiful, it makes all the difference, you know, time.

I still had time to enjoy my drink and smoke an illicit cigarette (I never could give up). Something fell in the bathroom, a bottle or maybe one of the candles that never manage to stay stuck in their holders. Maybe it was the stray cat that sauntered in and out as she pleased? I thought nothing more of it; why would I? I know we are meant to be scared in our homes here, but I refused to be vigilant to the point where it interfered with my enjoyment of life. I savoured another sip of my drink, honey and warm, ignoring the clammy feeling on my brow, the dampness in my armpits.

It hardly takes any time at all to learn how to be afraid.

I stood against the wooden counter, marble-topped for that was what I wanted, clean luxurious lines. I was a fan of decor magazines; if everything was going to hell outside may as well have a beautiful corner, a colour-coordinated and vanilla-scented soldier guarding against the imminent ugliness. The window afforded a view of my herb garden, where I had enjoyed tending and coaxing it to life. The ficus trees in their terracotta pots, pastel pink geraniums like elegant ladies in their Sunday best. The scarlet red Bougainvillea growing where she wished, a gentle guest to our balcony weekend breakfasts.

I wasn't listening anymore for any alarming sounds, my ears lulled to more pleasant pastimes and not cocked and pricked for any signs of danger. They were silent, the two of them were, stealthy and professional, I knew nothing of the danger coming up behind me, the strong determined hand pressing the gun to the back of my head.

Funny what you think when your life is threatened, when you are not sure if you will be spared or not. I forgot the mandarins I wanted to buy at the supermarket, but thought of a drawing Imogen had done in her first art class, how she was so proud of her efforts, even though the elephant's trunk was far too short for its body. I thought of William, cupping a plant in his hand, lowering it into the hole I dug last weekend.

I heard my heart hammer in my chest; running too fast to make the train you are about to miss doesn't even come close to the way it pounded inside of me. It was primal and terrified. If it could've hammered its way out of me, it would have.

They wanted keys to the safe. I had to think if we had ever had a safe and, if we did, where was it then. In the closet, in the wall, keeping jewellery and William's gun safe. I never cared much for guns, and William wanted to enroll the both of us in self-defense classes, target practise, the basics. I asked him why, arguing that it wasn't necessary. He lost interest, reasoning that maybe it wasn't needed. Now there was a gun in a safe I didn't know how to use. I asked them to be calm, and tried to imagine a painless end to this intrusion of my privacy, this intrusion on my life. Stay calm and collected, I told myself over and over again. The other man, unarmed and thin, handsome in a neglected hard life kind of way, jittery and nervous-looking rifled through the drawers, disconnected the sound system, ripping the speakers from the wall, pocketing my purse, my phone, my laptop. And tossed all he could find that was of value in a duvet cover (ours too). It was part of Imogen's tenth birthday present. She loved Strawberry Shortcake and here they were using it as a sack to carry our belongings away to who knows where, redistributing, selling, drug money? Who can blame anyone for wanting more?

All the time the gun was at my head, moving in a lethal slither to my temple, down to the whorl of my right ear. I remember the small scar running from his nose to the middle of his cheek. He tells me, "The pretty lady smells nice," and that his mother always stank of wine. So did my mother, stink of the drink, especially on weekends but what does that matter now and what would he care if we had something in common?

He came up close to the nape of my neck and took a deep breath, I showed him the safe, gave him the keys, everything. The other one, in his nervous fashion, continued to tour the house and make free with our things.

I should have had that last burglar bar put on the bathroom window. It was so easy to come in from the street and gain access to the alley. A quick jump over the wall and you would be in our garden. Why did I leave it? Because I wanted to see the garden in its full splendour from the bathroom. What stupidity, what ridiculous luxury in such times! Why couldn't I just realize it wasn't getting any better and steps had to be taken to feel a false sense of security? The man walked behind me, gun to my head, arm clamped on my arm which twisted up into the small of my back. I gave him all the keys I owned and he ransacked the safe. I was sad and angry that I had to lose my grandmother's wedding ring, but I would rather have made it out of my home alive, they could take anything.

"Just don't kill me."

He asked if there was a car in the garage. I told him that he would find one among the lawnmower, Imogen's old toys and her stroller. "It goes, gets you from A to B; it isn't fancy or anything, probably not what you expected but you are welcome to it." I can't believe what I am saying.

We went back to the kitchen and he wasn't comfortable with me being unbound, I could fight, I could kick him in the groin. I could foil his plans. With this black, heavy and cold gun pointed at my brain, I wouldn't have made any sudden moves.

I was tied to a chair, the one I always read in, especially in the mornings where it caught the winter light. Cable ties from his pocket and string he found in the kitchen drawer. Tight and immovable, my wrists, I thought, are bleeding. He was rough and suddenly more aggressive. He gagged my mouth with a dishtowel and duct tape. He brought the tape with him, prepared for any eventuality like a boy scout.

"Miss pretty smell lady," he hissed in my face, put the gun between my eyes, trailed it down my face as though he were stroking me with it, like we were old lovers and we were just playing at some far-out sex fantasy.

He traced the outline of my breasts with that cocked and loaded gun. It had to have been. Had the gun lain on his bedside table, did he shove it into his pants on the way out, what was he doing, what were they doing before they decided this?

My heart changed its rhythm to even more frantic beats, I was swimming in adrenaline, which doesn't help much if there is nowhere to fly to and only the useless fear to feel. He grabbed at my breasts, pawing and mauling them. The chair wasn't comfortable, how would he manage what he wanted to do, me sitting and tied up as I was? I thought, maybe it was just a game, his modus operandi to let me know who is boss, just to humiliate me a little. He possessed an incredible strength. I thought he must be on something, looking into his dead eyes, eyes that wouldn't soften over anything. He held the gun to my temple, it grazed and bruised the vulnerable skin found there; he leaned with his arm on the chair and undid his zip. I spotted his penis, skew and semi erect, it lay against the inside of my thigh, slimy, touching my skin. I didn't have any pants to pull down or buttons to fuss with, only a bathrobe that had come adrift when he tied me up and I didn't have the hands to pull it closed.

You have done this many times before, I thought, many before you have done it, accommodated this, felt this. It is the story we expect, the history we know well. My legs were still free, he had neglected to restrain them and I kicked as best I could at his sensitive parts with my knee. This infuriated him and he punched me hard in the face, my head spun and the room reeled around me, my skull throbbed. He punched me again for good measure and said, "Make no trouble, miss pretty." I had an urgent desire to urinate, my eyes watered and my bladder burned, I knew I was shaking, from some deep place inside of me, it was different to being cold on the surface, my muscles were tight and sore, no part of me wasn't terrified. He forced my legs open with practiced and horrifying ease, he half crouched, half lay on top of me, his knee grinding into my thigh, the gun ever visible and sneering, hissing, howling like hell must do in my face. What was this man doing here inside of me, in and out like a machine, tearing and scraping at my insides and his friend, he invited, called to from the other rooms or passage in the house, where had he been, what had he got for his trouble, was it worth it?

I had gone beyond feeling terrified, my body wanted to escape from itself but it was lodged into the gravity and articulation of its bones and ligaments. If only I could have torn myself away from my eyes, light years from here, come back when it is all over without having felt it.

The other smiled at me, one of those icy smiles that truly send shivers and waves of revulsion down your spine, like the chilling intent you glimpse in a predator. He hurt me more, taking care to make it as painful and invasive as possible; he had found my organs, pushing through what got in his way, up and up and up. Then he got off of me, hurriedly tucking his spent, limp penis back into his underpants.

They both laughed at me, an awful resonant cacophony of power gone mad, looking at me with the dishtowel in my mouth, trying to make a sound loud enough for someone gentle to hear, someone human; they were truly pleased with the helplessly fucked picture they had created.

I stank of sweat and fear and my middle twisted in and over itself, like intense menstrual cramps, the kind that would leave me doubled and biting pencils in half. I felt incredibly nauseous and got sick, as I was tied right back to the chair I couldn't really lean forward and I choked as I got sick, I coughed and spluttered trying to feel my lungs into breathing, trying to stop thinking that I would die.

They said that I was disgusting and, yes, I should choke, I deserved to.

"Shall we shoot her?"

"Yes, I think so, the bitch will put us away."

"Yes kill her kill her kill her bitch, stupid *poes*." They tossed a coin, and the one with the smile got the honour of killing me. I couldn't feel my heart anymore, it was beating like a small woodland animal's would, fast, an insect's wings, where there is no more fear to feel, something gives in, something breaks and blurs and you're just watching from a serene and peculiar distance. Should you survive it, your body would never be the same again.

They shot me in the leg first, testing the gun maybe or having fun with the idea of killing somebody, teasing me, it hardly made any sound. My leg was on fire, and they laughed.

"*Ja*, its sore getting shot. I got one in the leg and lung, lucky for you, miss pretty, I didn't die."

He sniffed hard, hawked and spat at my face.

He came close to me, I could see the stubble on his cheeks, the pimple on his chin, and suddenly I felt like laughing, how very absurd this all was, I thought, a pimple on his chin! I imagined him squeezing it in the mirror later, wherever he lived, in some bathroom mirror, when all of this was over. I didn't laugh, though, I thought I might still have some bargaining power left, and I didn't want to anger them, make their tempers flare up again, but what could be worse than

14

this? Where were their boundaries, how far and to what barbaric ends could they take themselves to and me with them?

The gun rammed between my eyes was taken away, the gun in his hand was shown around the room, as if he was having a casual conversation, gesticulating. They spoke to each other in Afrikaans. One of them had wanted to go and fetch the spoils first, not waste time climbing stairs and lugging it down after they have just shot someone.

He gave the gun to his partner and left. He knew where he was going in my home. The one left behind stared at me, made obscene gestures with the gun, rubbing it up and down with his free hand. "*Ja,* you got us good, us pretty boys."

I was afraid of wetting myself, it took all my voluntary power over the involuntary not to while they were having their way with me, raping me. It feels boundless in my mouth, to think of such a word, formless, invisible and undone, as if a threshold inside of me had been crossed and all turns and sours into madness from now on.

Well, I had already vomited all over myself, nothing much more to do then, after that. I couldn't hold it anymore and I let it go, warm and stinging down my legs. The relief was almost euphoric, soaking into the floral fabric of the chair. I would have to throw it away, no use trying to get that smell out, no use walking by it everyday reminding me of the day I almost made it out alive and well. He smiled at me, horrible and cold, when he saw the urine trickling down the wooden legs of my death chair. Why were they stalling so, enjoying it all so much? I wanted to break loose, I wanted to have the strength of armies, transform into Godzilla, break them like toothpicks between my claws; the wound in my leg was weakening me, and I could see a dark sticky pool of blood staining the carpet around me. My mouth felt dry and all I wanted was a drink of water, cool against my lips, I could think of a plan then, a way out. I gathered all I had left from my ragged and blurry edges for one last try at freedom and frantically moved my wrists. The cable ties had cut into them but I didn't feel it anymore, I thrashed in the chair, screaming from my bound and shut mouth.

The gun was at my head again and then, thinking his friend was taking too long, the man was tired of waiting, tired of playing. He put the gun between my legs and pushed it in as far up as it could go. Yes, that hurt. I remember how it felt, its foreign metal shape finding new ways to terrify me. He looked at me, right through my wide eyes and said nothing as he pulled the trigger and emptied the gun inside of me. I looked at the clock, watched the second hand, the minute hand as my insides were blown to pieces, as they tried to find their way back to their original places, as they tried to remember what their functions were, as they knew they were dying. It must have been almost instant, but it dragged on and on, the feeling of life ceasing, collapsing in on itself in profound spasms of agony.

Dying was nauseating too, like being on a hurtling roller coaster, as you struggle with G forces that your body isn't used to. As if you were travelling so very fast out of yourself and not knowing where you were headed. Pulled through wormholes, fantastic electric colours, further and further away. But I had only made it to the living room ceiling, pressed against it, trying to find a way through but nothing opened for me.

I don't know where my body is as I cannot feel it anymore, the way I am used to feeling it, only the shape of what it was, like having dead limbs and then pins and needles. My arms feel huge, my legs too small, I feel stretched like an elastic band and nothing obeys my will. How long will I be up here, stuck to the ceiling like a gecko? My vision can't be trusted either and everything has an eerie glow around it. Everything shimmers.

I could see him, the man who killed me, looking at me briefly, the dead me in the chair, looking at the mess he had made, pieces of me on the wall, something unidentifiable and blue-black on his face which he rubbed at furiously with his sleeve. I know he didn't know what he had done, he was trying to comprehend it, but his eyes couldn't take it in. He shouted to his friend, swore at him to hurry up. The friend came running with Imogen's Strawberry Shortcake duvet, they struggled with the bunch of keys, to find the car key. I could see by their faces that they were disappointed. Did they expect a luxury sedan? William was using the one they would've wanted that evening. They got in anyway, throwing the duvet in the back, breaking some of the things they had stolen, I am sure. The one who had won the toss said it wasn't fair, he had been ready to kill me and why did the other have to go and spoil the moment by being stupid.

The one who couldn't wait said, "*Jou poes, jou ma se poes. Fok*, it was my turn anyway to kill somebody, you know *mos* how it works!" I thought how boring language can become.

So they left my house with me dead in it, cussing and cursing, lighting cigarettes as they backed out the drive and made the tyres skid on the tar in the street. No one had heard a thing and if they had they wouldn't have come looking to see if everything was all right. I was not all right, I was bleeding like a slaughtered animal. I was going irretrievably mad from the pain but no one came looking. I would have to ride this out, wait till I was truly disconnected from my body, wait for William to come back from his ridiculous retirement party, holding his complimentary company cufflinks in his hand. I would have to carry on talking to myself, calming myself and learning the process of being dead.

2

WILLIAM NOTICES SOMETHING IS WRONG, the open garage door, the gate depending outwards from its hinge onto the sidewalk.

William thinks, "Sarah wouldn't leave the house exposed like this, would she? Maybe she craved something sweet and went to the supermarket, for a mandarin maybe? She had mentioned them, saying that they were at their sweetest and juiciest now. Wedges of sunshine, she called them. Maybe she thought to meet me at the restaurant rather, like a date when we were younger, creating a pleasant buzz of sexual anticipation."

He notices the tyre marks in the road as he gets out of his maroon Volvo. An unnerving feeling winds its way through his bloodstream, quickens his breath. He trips over Imogen's old tricycle, wonders what it is doing on the floor, its frame buckled as if someone has driven over it. He wipes his brow with his handkerchief and puts it back into his chino pocket. He takes a step through the side door that leads into the entrance hall of the house. He is met with chaos, papers and books strewn across the floor, stereo connections, a tangle of wires, nails and screws from the drawer that keeps such things no one ever knows where to put. His mouth dries and he swallows hard, his stomach dropping and falling to some disbelieving urgent place, his bowels feel loose, his hands, calloused and broad, begin to shake.

He calls my name and the silence like a maw shouts back at him. He walks through the hallway and is met with more of our belongings turned inside out and on their heads; ornaments have been smashed into pieces and his boots grind them into the floor as he takes step after dreadful step.

He turns into the open living room-kitchen and sees me sitting in my chair. Something stops him from saying hello to me, stops him from walking up to me and kissing me, stops him from telling me he shouldn't have wasted his time going to that party, that he was bored out of his mind. He is desperate to comprehend the image before him, but his brain won't let him, it howls and screams from its colossal depths, its secrets, fold upon fold unravelling in hysterical jagged angles. The image, the connection, fires like a groan withheld, catapulting him into the vacuum of space and incomprehension. William's legs give way beneath him and he finds himself on his knees and he is not sure what to do next. His mouth opens and closes but no sound comes out of him. He leans against the couch, an over-sized piece that looks like a soft cloud. He covers his eyes, his guts twist and he runs to the bathroom, making it just ahead of his vomit. It is the first sound that has come out of his body since calling my name. He rinses his mouth, splashes his face, something that I wasn't able to do. Something practical pushes him into overdrive, in an attempt to avoid what has happened in his home, some calming thought that he could just call an emergency service and I would be okay. Thinking that it was just a little accident. This lie gets him from one room to the next.

He remembers where the phone is, he walks to it and picks up the receiver in shaking hands and dials the police. It rings for far too long and he starts to wonder if there is anyone there at all, will he be put through to an electronic voice, rerouted or disconnected? An uninterested voice eventually answers and asks for his address. William tells him that his wife is dead, there has been a robbery. His voice loses its usual even tone and breaks, disobeys him. He clears his throat, and breathes in deeply.

"A car will come," the voice tells him. It didn't know how long but soon. His wife is dead, of that he is certain, he knew it right away but he wanted to believe deep in his limbic brain that his instinct was wrong. He presses the panic button; the security company will come at least. Somebody will come.

The police arrive minutes after the security company, and the house swarms with blue and khaki uniforms. William thinks he is late for his dinner, he constantly looks at his watch, avoiding the sight of his dead wife in her favourite chair.

The police are suspicious that he isn't hysterical, or crying even, just standing there contemplating the time, his body trembling.

An inspector with a paunch is assigned the task of taking his statement. He has dark rings under his eyes and apologizes for William's loss. But wonders where he was when this happened.

He shouldn't have been anywhere, why didn't he stay, make up some excuse to miss his own retirement send-off, like "I know I am going to lose my wife, know she is going to die a horrible and humiliating death if I don't stay at home."

He clears his throat again and tells the inspector he was at the office, "There was a small party; I am leaving after 25 years of service."

The inspector leans in towards William, crosses something out on the paper, rubs his eyes with his thick fingers. "You have an alibi, then, people who can vouch for your whereabouts. That is good, what is the name of the company, the address?"

William tells him in a disconnected manner, "It is in a lovely part of Cape Town. My office used to look out to a corner of the ocean. I was there 25 years; can you believe that, Inspector? A long time to be in one place. Sarah and I we were going to do all the things we never had the time or the energy to do."

The inspector smiles halfway into his cheeks, it is more of a smirk, something that isn't quite sure why William is telling him these things.

"You found her, yes, like this?"

"Yes, I came back home and the doors were open and I knew something was wrong, then saw the mess in the house. Sarah, yes I found her." William glances in my direction and that of a policewoman beginning the process of collecting evidence around my body, dropping parts of me into vials. They would take me away, put me on some cold metal slab and continue the investigation in a more thorough fashion, away from sensitive and unaccustomed eyes. Eyes like William's. The inspector doesn't think to take the shocked and dazed William into another room to take his statement. Right there on the couch in the living room-kitchen is as good a place as any.

He feels his stomach lurch again and swallows hard, dry retches. The inspector doesn't seem fazed by the condition of my body; he has seen this before. But William hasn't and he wants to scream; he needs to scream like a crazed rabid animal, and bites his bottom lip instead, grinding it into silence. The efficiency, the almost Sunday normality of how they are going about this tragedy disturbs him. Someone dusts the fallen and broken objects for fingerprints. The woman with me and others stand around in the passage, leaning against the walls, asking questions amongst themselves, what are they talking about? Maybe something on the television that they want to watch. Are they hungry or thirsty? Can't they wait to be gone and leave him alone in his house, alone without his wife? This is a loneliness he could never have imagined. He had always wanted to die first, knowing that he didn't have what it took to go on without me, slipping away quietly in his sleep and I would wake up and carry on planting flowers and small trees, making it all beautiful.

"Did you see anyone? Did anyone tell you that they saw anything?" The inspector is clearly desperate for a lead.

"No, I didn't see anyone, no neighbours came to me." Now he notices those same neighbours milling about in the street outside. They want to know what has happened, they are ready to offer their opinion and add to the feeling of anxiety and hysteria. They will offer empty condolences, relieved that it wasn't them or the ones they loved. Some are in their dressing gowns, some stand with mugs of tea or coffee in their hands, trying to glean information from the police. William wants to run out and brandish a shotgun at them and tell them to leave, to leave him and me alone. Is there no respect for the dead or the grief-stricken, what is wrong with all of them? But William stays where he is, listening to the dull inspector's questions, painfully aware of the gun on his hip. They all have guns on their hips and it makes him nervous and scared, afraid for himself, he wishes the questions were over, he wishes he didn't have to see me, being wheeled out on to the street and into a van and the chair splattered with blood and other parts of her.

"What items were stolen, Mr...," the inspector moves his eyes to the top of his page, "... Jenkins?"

William has no idea, what does it matter, he only wants his wife back, alive with him for the rest of his life.

"The usual, I guess, inspector. It wasn't something I noticed when I came inside!"

"Well, we can get a list later, as you discover the stolen items." The inspector blows his nose and apologizes for his cold.

William stares at his hands, feeling infinitely small, as if he isn't made up of anything substantial and solid and no one would know the difference anyway, if he was there or not.

"Is there anything else you can think of? No matter how unimportant you think it is, it could help the investigation." William's head pounds and he tries to think of anything, any possible thing that could help, but he comes up empty.

"Well, if something comes back... You know the shock can affect your memory, if you remember any detail, call me." The inspector smiles a little wider this time, and adjusts the gun on his hip as he stands up, closing the folder over William's statement. The police file out, pushing their bulletproof frames through the front door in tandem. The blue flashing lights vanish from the early morning street; the neighbours go back into their homes as the excitement is now over. William closes and locks his door on the world and pours himself a Scotch, one of the few things in the house that are still intact, warm and comforting in its transparent bottle. He will find more whole and present things as the days pass, just now in this moment there is nothing that doesn't look lost or broken. The Scotch makes a clinking cracking sound as it splashes over the ice. He drinks deeply from the plastic picnic cup he found, bright and disarming on the kitchen floor. He pours another, remaining in the kitchen, not sure where to take his body, now that the routine is gone, the delicate essential places on a clock's face. He sinks to the floor, leaning against the stove, sipping slowly now at his drink, souring his stomach. The silence hurts and whines in his ears like white noise, what would they be doing now, sleeping like spoons in their bedroom after making love? He can't torture himself with the ifs of their planned evening. I am dead and he is here in our kitchen drinking because he can't bring himself to look into the gaping hole of the hours he has now.

William's first night was the hardest, while I sat watching, an invisible observer from that couch we liked so much. I managed to gather a certain amount of control over my body or not body (death is confusing) and came down from the dizzying height of the ceiling, as they wheeled my body into the street and into the van. Where are you going without me, Sarah? At least the murderous agonizing pain was gone, only a disconcerting tingle left, not quite numbed.

I watched William empty that three quarter bottle of Scotch in miserable determination to pass out cold, but sleep eluded him. I watched him pace the floor back and forth, watched him sway and crash into the furniture, breaking things already broken, emptying the cupboards of plates, smashing them against the walls, my husband tormented by the savagery of his loss, inconsolable and unable to weep. It is the first time I have witnessed such violence in him, such cauterized emotion. He had never been the temperamental man, the aggressive man, a man that gave himself fully and with sad abandon to alcohol. He had been enraged once when he caught Imogen making out with some boy in the garage amongst her childhood fluffy toys. Lifeless, glazed witnesses to her curious sexuality. He had frogmarched him out into the street, with Imogen wailing after William that she loved the boy.

"I was just kissing him, Dad, what is the big deal, have you never been in love?"

"You don't know what love is yet," he had said to her. "If it was up to me you would never know; next thing you will be telling me is that we are going to be grandparents!"

The awkward boy, his feet shod in shabby sneakers, stood on the sidewalk not knowing what to do next.

"It was just a kiss, Dad!"

"That kind of kissing escalates into adolescent tragedy and missed opportunity, a wrecked life, Imogen!"

She turned away from him in frustration, her long hair the colour of mahogany, swishing behind her as though it too could be annoyed and angered. Back into the house she went to flop onto her bed in exasperation;

she did that often, it was a new idiosyncrasy, and wholly unpleasant. What happened to the sweet little girl who thought he was the entire world and could answer all her questions?

William went out to the boy where he stood, all glum and sullen, looking a little afraid that her father might physically harm him, like a hillbilly with a loose finger on the trigger. He backed himself into the boundary wall hoping to disappear.

"You got money to get yourself home, take a train or something?"

"Mmm, no Mr...," because he had neglected to find out Imogen's surname. He thought "sir" sounded better.

"No, Sir, got no cash on me." The boy lived close enough to walk home, but he could get something out of this, a loose cigarette at the corner cafe, a cool drink maybe.

William worried his pocket for a R5 coin and put it into the eager and sweaty hand of the boy.

"You know son, I know."

A man will always welcome another younger male into the fold by calling him "son", finding the common ground, the common shared urge that resides in their crotches. The boy felt more at ease, knowing just what Imogen's father was on about.

"That urge comes strong and fast, son, you think you going to burst if you don't get to know what it is about. Take your time, don't go getting yourself into trouble and don't go having urges around my daughter. Do we understand each other?"

"Yes sir, we understand each other."

Of course, the boy became part of our family for

a few months, with William being ever vigilant with curfews and open doors and always having to know where Imogen was. It was sweet to see her holding the boy's hand, looking at him as though she loved him, and then nursing her broken heart when he found another girl that was willing to go all the way.

"See," William would tell me, "I knew he was up to no good and possessed no values or distinguishing moral fibre. What an insult he is to our daughter, she deserves better anyway!"

"She is only fifteen. William, how many girlfriends did you have before you married me? Imogen was just one person in his life as he was in hers." He rubbed the stubble on his chin in the dark, the sound of fine sandpaper on skin.

"Guess you are right," he conceded, "I just hate to see her sad and what if we were just lucky, what if this is all a sign of things to come and stay for her: doomed relationships?"

"People have lived without love, people have lived with a lot less than we can imagine, William."

No, I cannot say I have ever put too much stock in love, never thinking that it changed much, that one feels it on the surface, something that is lived around selfishly and not inside of and my husband dependent and generous like a puppy. Always happy and uncomplicated. I am not sure how, but somehow we fitted enough to stay married.

Of course he never said to Imogen, "I told you so." He took her out for ice-cream instead, pinching her downcast cheeks. "Cheer up, sweetheart, plenty of fish in the sea."

William, father and husband, is reduced to a shivering helpless shape, pressed close to a kitchen cabinet, the picnic cup fallen from his hand and the bottle drained. His head is spinning and the first signs of light begin to appear. I lean against his shoulder and he succumbs to sleep right where he is, in his shoes and office clothes. I want to think that it is me that lets him find the stillness enough to sleep.

I plan to keep my routine or the semblance thereof. I step out into the garden and inspect the plants for wilted leaves, blights, unwanted insects. It doesn't matter to me that I can't touch them or make any difference to what is affecting them. I know William will let the garden go. I can only watch it wither, all my hard work, all my love, for nothing. So this is what it comes to, nothingness, and if I had the eyes to cry I would.

I can't be here now and I leave William sleeping, his mouth agape on the kitchen floor. He is going to have an awful hangover when he finally wakes up.

The street looks the same yet I expect it to be different. It could be that my murder never happened and Mrs Watson next door is watering her roses in her floppy pink sun hat. I greet her out of habit but I get no reply. She curses the aphids instead, squashing them between her thumb and her forefinger. I tell her she should use a mixture of dish-washing liquid and tobacco. That will sort them out, I shout at her. She swats a fly from her face and turns the green watering hose off. She would have been one of the first of those neighbours outside complaining about the ruckus, saying, "I knew there were drug dealers here, plain as day, selling their illicit wares on the street!" On closer inspection, from the unnerving blue lights to the police in and out of our home, she would sadden a little, make empty statements like, "Well, I told them to sort out that easy access to their garden, they were far too lax, Inspector, I warned them, I got a Fort Knox system, not even a mite can get in, oh it is a shame, too terrible. How will we sleep at night now? What a country to be living in!"

This could be liberating, I think to myself, nobody hearing me. I could say anything I liked; all the things manners had prevented me from saying.

I can ignore the tired dark rings around her eyes, her powdered wrinkled face; I can ignore the fact that she is old and set in her ways like a shiftless boulder. She should know though, shouldn't she, someone should tell her!

I gather up all the voice I think I have and come right up to her face, she bends down to wind up the hose.

Hey, Mrs Watson, you are a cantankerous old bag, you still call the man who works in your garden "the boy". You still give him coffee out of a separate tin mug, you lock the shed behind him, scared he will make off with your things, feed him that leftover stale bread, and the food in the fridge *just* inside the sell-by date; horrible woman you are!

Mrs Watson goes inside, wiping her muddy shoes on her welcome mat, rubbing a gnawing pain in the small of her back with a liver-spotted hand. She didn't hear a damn thing I said or hear anything at all.

I feel lighter having said it, anyway, feel a little whoop of delight tingle in the air around me. If I had the legs to skip I would.

I feel like taking a taxi to the city, haunting the streets, slipping in and out of shops, lying prostrate in the field of flowers on Adderly Street, listening to toothless women my age calling me sweetheart: "What will it be today, lovey, sunflowers, special winter roses?" Well, yes, if they could see me that is what they would say. Watching what people do while alive, as I try to forget all these familiar places, what they do with life, discard it into the nearest tip and then lament over where the hell it got to, or those lucky ones sailing and soaring, drinking chai lattes brought to them by waiters with Afro hairstyles? The ones that know how to make the best of division and disparity.

It doesn't matter much that the taxi is full, as I fit snuggly between the curvaceous bosom of a laughing woman, and the coat-sleeves of an old reed-thin man who smells of tobacco and shack smoke. A sticker above the driver's head says, *No heavyweights in the front.* A hip-hop tune blares full blast from speakers which are molded neatly into the taxi's sides. A prayer in gold letters to Allah dangles from the rear-view mirror, the driver, with a sliver of gold flashing from his teeth, curses someone in the traffic.

"*Sies*!" the thin man next to me says, shifting uncomfortably on the bones of his backside.

I laugh, laugh because I am a dead woman travelling in a taxi to the Grand Parade, one of the most dangerous places to disembark from public transport. Taking one's life in one's hands is the new sport.

A voice says, "What are you laughing at, nothing funny here!"

I turn around to see who has heard me, yet no one looks my way. People still speak on their cell phones, or are asleep against the window. The woman next to me fusses in her cleavage with her money pouch. I turn to the man next to me and he is looking straight at me with grey watery eyes.

"You can hear me?"

"*Ja*, why wouldn't I be able to?"

I don't know what to make of this, maybe he is special, one of those John Edward types who can hear the dead and cross over, or maybe he is just dead like I am. My mother used to watch those circus shows with obsessed interest.

"I want to write in, Sarah," she'd say. "I got a mind to go on that show and have a word or two for that son of a bitch father of yours. Got a word for him, how do we write in? Gone to hell I'm sure of it, got a hot poker permanently wedged in his fat arse!" Then she would drain her glass and pass out, sleep well into a late night porn film with a buxom blond bouncing on top of a man.

Screaming.

That was then, but she had fallen victim to an obscure church group when she went for her first AA meeting. The high priestess in a pink cardigan and highlighted hair could see the lost-sheep-look in my mother's eyes and took her under her wing.

"The Lord made wine," she said, "meant to drink and so we shall, we don't need these meetings quashing our very natures! No use in stinting ourselves all the way, cutting it out like a tumour." She had been a battered wife too, just like my mother had been and still was in her head. And sometimes she said they deserved their escape, that some things have to be worked around and accommodated, things like pain.

Work it with love was their slogan, the point being that the drink should never escalate to self-hatred, those all-night hard liquor binges were strictly out of bounds and contrary to love and the Lord wouldn't want that.

"The Lord is kind and understands," they would chant, over and over again, like a mantra, over a 5 litre box of cheap sweet plonk. At least my mother's drinking had a purpose to it now, its own sanctified passages to gather strength from.

"You are not fooling me, Mom," I said to her.

"Oh Sarah. Stop fussing so much; why so hard and intolerant?"

"You are replacing one crutch with another without letting go of the first, using each to justify the other!"

"Semantics dear. You would be drinking too!"

"You think I didn't live it with you, do you really think that?"

"Sarah, water under the bridge now. Go on, get your mother a chocolate, have a fierce craving for one of those fine imported praline swirls." She always did that when the conversation rushed to where she didn't want it to go, to foreign lands.

Not too long before this happened to me she complained about that woman, wondering about the sincerity of her religious intentions.

"She brings a little collection box, you know, all covered in cheap wrapping paper, like a kid had made it in play-school. She says it's for the fold, to spread the word, man can't live on bread alone and all that."

"Did you ever see this fold, Mother? I mean, was there an actual congregation?"

"Well, we were about six women once, all met at

33

my house. Some all smart and just stepped out of the beauty salon, others in shabby jerseys and bargain bin finds. We spoke, made plans for a way forward for our new church. Can I call it that?"

"Not even close. Of course she's a charlatan, Mother. Didn't you know that straight away?

"Are you still here?"

The man next to me peers into my face, and I can imagine rivers in the wrinkles of his face.

Well, yes, at least I think I am. Are you here?"

"Not really, don't know, I am still getting used to it, only been two weeks and I still go to work thinking I have some bricks to lay but I can't catch them. It is sad that you have to die to feel at your best, your strongest, I can imagine putting up a building in one day, walls and walls and higher up the ladder I would climb and at the top I would wear a tie and a suit and people would listen to me."

He doesn't look very strong, looks as if he would buckle under the slightest whisper of wind. I want to ask him what had happened to him, but wonder if that is breaking some code or etiquette of the newly dead.

"R5 is all I had in my pocket, and one cigarette, and I lay dead in the street like an old goat slit at the throat. They came out of nowhere from the darkness like spirits! I think why, why as my blood runs out of me, what did I do wrong to anger my ancestors, that I should be taken like this?"

I find that same old sympathy form on my lips and escape, "I am sorry." Who can blame the living then for saying the only thing possible.

"*Ja,* nothing but dead stones in this place, it is very

sad. What happened to you?"

I don't know what to tell him, I can hardly quantify it myself. "I was shot in my home. A robbery."

"Ha! Those tsotsis, lazy and crazy, a bad mix. Happens to everyone, no lines anymore, no colour. That's the one good thing from it. We all have a story between being dead and alive. Our stories bring our truths together. Then the stories, they are loved enough to tell again."

I turn his words over and over, try to make sense of them. One person's heroic story is another's blatant display of cruelty and prejudice and, I would think, nothing to be proud of.

Could all of this be the new patriotism, the equality of fear but no one involved prepared to give up their stories, but hold them close rather because loosening the grip betrays the memories of those gone? This is who we were, this is who we are. And everything falls down through the unspoken blank side of truth.

Those who refuse to leave, those who dare the night and shadowy places, even if they die trying. Or would we all leave if we could and leave the stories to fend for themselves, trading the blue open and sunny sky for something else?

I see the beginning of tears form in his eyes. I wonder how he does this, are there levels of expertise in death too or do I cry and not know it? Do I need another dead person to say, "Yes, I can see you are crying"?

I touch his hand and am relieved beyond the living ideas of tenderness to find that his hand is warm.

The taxi reaches its destination, and its occupants tumble out, clutching their belongings to their chests, walking briskly as if they know exactly where they are going and would fight if any pickpocket or knife-wielding shadow were to stop them.

"It is easy to go freely among the fear, don't you think?" The man with the warm hand stands casually against a sign that warns against public drunkenness, urinating in public and general antisocial behaviour. I have already spotted three men relieving themselves against a wall and a little girl squatting, her mother trying to hide her with her skirt.

"Nothing can happen to us anymore. Yes, it is good to feel this way!"

I am not convinced, I still feel too much part of the world to be indifferent to it.

"Ha, my friend, it gets easier by the hour, you will see."

Then he is gone, dissolved into thin air like the real ghost that he is.

People say that when they see ghosts or phenomena they can't explain, "It was there one minute, gone the next and the hair on my arms stood on end, and my dog, Mitzi, was having a fit over something, you know animals know, can sense these things." I wondered if I did that, could do that, become a story someone told their best friend over their latte.

I went to one of my favourite coffee shops, and sat down on the wooden window sill, watched people come and go. I had nothing better or more important to do.

Two women sat near me, at a round wobbly table. The one who looked bothered or annoyed wedged a folded serviette underneath its legs. She flicked her blond hair from her face and said to her friend who looked tired and bored.

"Claire, I swear I am not shitting you. Like, I saw this shape like a soggy blob of cotton wool and then it just disappeared." A soggy blob, this is what I have become, not something poetically descriptive like a diaphanous nymph seen cavorting in the Adderly Street fountain, luring the lovelorn and lost to come and play.

Claire thought the Fear was getting to her friend, caused by the forced removal of her new cell phone while a penknife was held to her throat.

The waiter brought them their order, two tall skinny lattes. He didn't smile.

"Man, I am over that, no big deal, happens to everyone, but I miss the damn phone. What's the use of it, really, if you can't flash it around?"

"Not much use at all," Claire replied with a marked lack of interest, as she has remained faithful to the land-line. She sucked on her cigarette, enjoying the unseasonably warm winter day, as was I.

The conversation descended into one of God and religion and the paranormal. Claire's friend was desperate to explain how she saw me. "What if someone or, freakier still, s*omething,* is observing what we do down here, cataloging our behaviour into a gigantic folder, just waiting for us to screw up and then, zap, you got a fire bolt up your ass or you see a ghost!"

Claire replied that humanity isn't interesting enough to invest such energy. "We are alone darling, nothing more to say about it."

The Afrocentric tunes lay back in the upright chairs of the coffee shop, inhaling incense, spilling into the street. So, this is beaded and printed Africa as we like to show it to the tourists, put it in your pocket to take it home with you.

I am still hungry as I never got to eat that dinner with my husband. My middle, at least where I think my middle still is, gnaws at me with an unaccustomed ravenous hunger. I can smell the coffee and vanilla cakes in the street I am now on, the fresh loaves in the bakery windows. I wish I could take one bite, one sip. One last try at being alive. Something sticky and cholesterol-laden. Would it matter now? I could smoke cigarettes one after the other, drink like my mother and never feel my lungs harden or my liver rot. There would be definite advantages to this if I could get my lips around filter-tipped Virginia leaf, or secret a bottle of the finest malt from a liquor store. I can imagine it instead, imagine what it used to taste of, what the smoke felt like in my lungs, the small pleasure of biting into something sweet.

I can see Table Mountain from where I am standing, that ancient graceful lady and all of Cape Town's disparity fretting and niggling in her lap like a disappointed child. She is still beautiful from this detached vantage point and today clouds peaked like whipped cream rush down her sides. It might rain later, a hard driving rain, I always liked to hear the rare soft rolls of thunder, and watch the rain scour everything clean and almost new. The dead man was right, it does become easier by the hour and I don't have to feel that afraid anymore or scared at all, really. I can move around Cape Town's streets freely, as though I had every right to.

I can watch the tourists wearing their digital cameras around their necks (how many times do we have to warn them?) bothered by wild, aggressive street children and older and sadder beggars.

I know I am another statistic in the police folder, as the strong arm of the law sips at its morning coffee. I am only another person gone from Cape Town's illusively protective lap. I have some meaning and no meaning at all.

My worst fear has already happened, though I didn't survive it, it can only get better from here. My anger a hard stone, honed to a fine edge though I am still learning the rules of being dead.

I begin to miss William, while feeling small and insignificant in this wide sprawling place I can't touch. As I said, those feelings stay. I take another taxi home, for the fun of it, because I don't need to get anywhere and it would make no difference if I never arrived at a destination. I brave the maniacal drive through rush hour, the speakers blaring full blast and all the drivers bad tempered and tired. No one speaks to me or sees me this time. I make my way back to my home down the familiar neglected streets, side stepping the dog and human faeces on the side walk, thinking I still have to. I could step right into it, feel it squish between my imaginary toes and be no worse off for the revolting experience. I could tread it into the house and it would leave no marks or smell. It is an exhilarating experience moving through walls and doors, I get to see how things really are, see the dead wood cells of our front door, the mortar of our walls that makes way for me, push enough and anything will make way.

The storm is gathering as I predicted out on the sodium streets, the air is ionized like the atmosphere must have been in the beginning of the world when the dust aggregated and swirled to make something out of nothing much. So much of nothing at all that I can look at my husband sitting at his desk staring at the telephone. William wonders if he should call someone. How on earth did we get here? My heart filled with a rank stench, the stench of nothing being fair. I wonder if he can smell my anger. I wonder if he knows that I can see him, wiping his brow, running his fingers through his hair again and again. He looks sick, like he has developed a sudden terminal disease. He is still in the same clothes I left him in this morning.

He musters up the strength to punch in the numbers. Imogen.

He is greeted by her answering machine. Her voice fresh and confident, as though the owner is always doing something important, perhaps discussing issues such as the politics of gender or genetically modified food or neo-colonialism. The groups I was in never discussed anything more important than what to prepare for supper, swapping recipes, or what our children were doing.

I must have at university, but I can't remember it. Most women at that time went to university to find a husband, it was an in-between state till their real roles of wife and mother began. They never thought that they could take their studies further. Well, that's how I thought about it. My group of graduates idolized the ones that went further, feeling they were something we could only hope to aspire to as we changed our children's nappies and clucked over our new husbands. Or we could take a secretarial course, learn how to type, painted nails clicking on the keys, learn how to file things away and speak on the telephone in a sing song voice.

I took to writing short stories for a time, to stave off impending boredom. I wasn't particularly bored with how my life had turned out, only bored with myself. I felt that I lacked the imagination to become more or do more. Tidy television commercials would liken it to the idea of having one's own space to think, away from the crying children, and the dependent husband who couldn't watch his own cholesterol level. In between spreading sandwiches with polyunsaturated fat you could escape to your little hermitage and feel more important, which in essence cancels the good intention into feeling patronized. My stories lay strewn in my 2x4 metres of space along with the other fleeting hobbies: pottery, flower arranging, acrylic painting. It is a disquieting feeling that that room represented something I forgot about, something I never got to. I had given it all up so easily to a world I thought everyone aspired to and had eventually. I enter it, here it is, this small room where I lost the world I wanted.

Imogen had no thoughts of a husband, not now anyway, and I stopped asking, resenting that she could just change the course of feminine history by saying "no", choosing something different.

Why could I never imagine doing that? Imogen left high school with top honours, went to university, and you could say I never saw her again. I lost count of the degrees she accumulated, the bursaries awarded to her, lost track of her life as it never seemed to leave the safety of the walls thick with ivy. She lectures and writes article upon article for academic journals. Now and then she will turn something out that her mother wants to read.

"Why can't you live in the real world, Imogen?"

"What is the real world, Mother?"

We were having one of our rare visits around a teapot and muffins that I had made fresh that morning. Her question caught me off guard, made me wonder, and soon enough even the question seemed absurd. If I concentrated long enough, I started to feel as though I was only tethered to this earth by a very fine string, I could float away at any time, unsure if I even existed and all that I had done didn't mean anything, not even to me. All was insubstantial and transient. A paper house with paper objects dressing up and dressing up again, waiting for something else to happen.

"I just don't know, Imogen, I had an idea, what we see around us I think, the tangible solid things, what makes everything matter and carry on!"

"All illusion, Mother, we choose a world we can live in, a world that makes sense to us. There are spinning globes in all of our heads and the continents and animals we find there will be different to the land on another's."

I decided my globe wasn't that interesting and a would-be explorer would miss it in the blink of an eye.

William doesn't know what to do with Imogen's recorded voice, he has never known what to do with telephones in general, keeping conversations clipped and to the point. He knows he can't leave a message telling her that her mother was murdered last night. He finds a middle ground and tells her to call him as soon as it was possible as it was urgent.

It isn't urgent anymore, I am already gone, there is nothing she can do about it.

He puts down the receiver and stares at it again. His hair is thinning, I never noticed that when I was alive, his scalp bare and geriatric in places, a real and present glimpse of the old man waiting to claim him.

The telephone rings and William is startled enough to move the chair he is in a few inches, pencils rolling to the floor, his arms flailing, a yelp of fright escaping from his mouth. He takes in a deep breath and answers. It would be almost comical if he didn't look so pathetic.

His friend, Scott Granger, is making a sympathy call. How Scott Granger knows before our own daughter baffles me. Scott always knows everything before anybody else does. Need a part for your car and Scott will find it for you, need a new house and he will give you someone's card. Scott says things like, "I will have my people call your people," in between playing squash in his neat white shorts and finding time to cheat on his wife.

William nods his head like a puppet, still in shock he tells Scott, "I can't talk now really. You understand don't you?" Scott must understand as the conversation ends with a "thank you for calling."

William throws the receiver back on its cradle, pours a drink from a bottle he has brought from the kitchen, I assume, or maybe he went out like that to the liquor store. Newly retired and a widower. A lethal combination, and I can't stop where he is going and who would blame him really? I know he loved me, even adored me.

Death is easier to accept when you are prepared for it, isn't it? If you know how much time you have with someone before a terminal illness slowly bears them away from you. You can prepare your insides for the eventual assault of loss. Natural causes. Or is a sudden heart attack no better, or waking up to your dead partner who left you while you were asleep?

Mrs Watson's husband went that way, in his sleep at 68 and she hasn't been the same since, growing more bitter and sour as the years pass by. She took a year to get out of her moth-eaten dressing gown, her house fell down about her, her cat starved till I fed her, her eyes huge and stricken in the mangy skull.

"She can eat a mouse or a rat, plenty of those in the streets, she doesn't need me anymore, she is just lazy and pampered, that is all. It's in her Persian blood, nothing to do but to look pretty!"

My eyes watered from the putrefying neglect Mrs Watson had now given herself over to with rigor and enthusiasm.

Her daughter and son-in-law came eventually, after I called saying that I was worried about her, that the situation was out of hand. The son-in-law stood with his hands in his pockets saying sensible things like, "Mother, it can't go on like this," his pager clipped to his thick leather belt, his wide retro tie resting on his growing paunch. The daughter gaping like a fish out of water at the dishevelled sight of her mother and her house, her high heels standing in something green and oozing, the leftovers of a long ago dinner.

She had a toughness about her, though, and took no notice of her mother's violent protestations when she forced her under the shower-head, using every bar of soap she could find in the house, scrubbing her mother's withered form with annoyance that softened into a hollow kind of sorrow when her mother giggled as she washed her feet. Husband outside on the porch checking his messages, sucking on a cigarette and fresh air, keeping an eye on his new luxury sedan.

Then the cleaners were called, able in their white starched overalls, and so the scouring and disinfecting began a room at a time. Mrs Watson emerged from her newly cleaned home in a fresh change of clothes, something pretty and understated under her gardening coat. She took to pruning the roses that had grown woody and vicious in her absence.

I saw her cut the gnarled dead stems as if she was performing intricate and delicate surgery on someone she loved, that the outcome of her attention was a barometer of her progress or her life.

"Did you miss me?" she kept on asking. "Yes, yes, I know. I have missed you too."

Does it matter, then, how we go, or just that we go?

I come behind William, imagine putting my arms around him, try to tell him it will be okay. We rock ourselves to the sound of the rain on the windows. He puts his head on the desk, studies a piece of lint and some 5-cent pieces, turns a pencil thumb over forefinger. The rain gathers momentum, furious and violent, tearing away from the clouds, hurtling down to our little spinning ball, and the trees curtsy in the gale force wind, their crowns teasing the tar of the street, torsos swaying and moving where they are, stuck where they are.

The phone rings again and this time William is so enamored with the objects on his desk that he hardly stirs, reaches blindly for the receiver, cradles it between his chin and his arm.

"Hello." His voice sounds thick and woozy, as though it was spinning in its own fog and he had no command over it anymore.

Imogen apologizes for not being there. He is telling her that it is, "OK, dear, all OK." He doesn't know how to tell her, he doesn't even know how to tell it to himself. There is a long, uncomfortable silence and William wonders if he could just sit here listening to his daughter's breathing and not say anything. Imogen holds on for as long as patience will allow her and I can hear her say, "Dad? DAD!"

"There was an accident, Imogen. I have some bad news. Well, not an accident. God, I don't know what to say, how to say it."

Bad news; what an inane thing to say. I would've said it better. Wretched news, something so fantastically and horrifically absurd, Imogen, you would never believe it, shouldn't believe it or accept it!

Imogen's voice grows louder and filled with rising apprehension. "Dad what is it? You're scaring me, what's going on?"

"It's your mother. There was a break-in." William's voice falters, trips over his words, dissolves into choked silence.

"What happened, Dad? Just tell me, please!"

William hates feeling weak, especially in front of his daughter, he is her father, he had shared the job of answering her questions, he has to know how to tell her, he has to be brave enough. He tenses his muscles, clenches his jaw around the words that threaten to blow the top of his head off.

"The intruders, they had a gun, shot her, I am sorry sweetheart but she didn't make it." He can hear

Imogen drawing in deep breaths, shallower, quicker and quicker, shorter and shorter.

"Imogen?"

"Dad, I have to go."

The phone goes dead in his ear. He didn't expect that response, he didn't know what to expect. This was foreign ground, an alien-inhabited landscape, an atmosphere made up entirely of ammonia, and temperatures that would melt the skin off your bones.

I see that he has written an appointment down for the cleaners on a crumpled piece of paper. They will arrive armed with bleach, industrial-strength carpet cleaners and polite detachment, wiping me out, making it all as it was before, early tomorrow morning. Not many crime scene cleaners around, I can't imagine anyone wanting to make a living out of cleaning the pulverized remains of others. Why has he neglected it? I would've been on my hands and knees with a wire brush just like my mother used to, cleaning up after everyone. I couldn't have stood the mess for a minute. I would have made our home right again before the day was out. He hasn't even thrown that chair out yet and I doubt he will. He is developing some morbid attachment to it.

He sidesteps it every time he has to go to the kitchen to look at food he isn't going to eat, holing himself up in his study, where he only has to worry about putting his books back on the shelves, ordering the desk drawers again. Is my sense of time questionable, am I being too hard on my newly single husband, expecting him to heal this sudden hole by the time the sun rises again? It feels like decades have passed, it feels like life has been very long and just a second lived at the same time. I don't know where I have been, nor where we could be possibly going, our separate ways, alone.

He pushes himself away from his desk and makes his way to our bedroom, taking the bottle with him. He gets under the covers, lying on his side and fumbles his way through the dark for the bedside light. He has forgotten to take his glass with him and chases a Valium with a gulp of Scotch straight from the bottle. I can see this makes him feel even more lost and hopeless. He will be on the street soon, he thinks, a man who loved his wife so much he couldn't live without her. "The loss turned his mind," all the old neighbours will say and they might bring him a solid meal on Sundays.

I watch him toss and turn and wait for sleep, the bed is too big for him, I know, and I can count on one hand the nights we've slept apart. He turns the light on and then off again, sipping Scotch and taking another Valium. A pain like that will need something that will make a horse lie down – something my grandmother would say, though her pain was only ever physical, life being too hard to worry about things like emotions.

"You have to harden up, Sarah," she always said. "No use crying over turned milk."

"Isn't it spilled milk?"

"Either way, you can't use it or you won't like it!"

Why haven't I seen her yet? She would have got bored hanging around in limbo and given her idle hands something to do, fashioned something out of heaven.

"A woman's work, Sarah, is never done, and that is the only truth if you are looking for one!"

Sleep eventually makes his anxious face slacken, takes him somewhere I can't follow, though the hum of love is omnipresent. I had thought that love would be enough one day, when it came to this. That you would catch sight of the real thing when you died and it would open your eyes for the first time.

Still, there is the same wall, the same hindrance of never quite being with another, always annoyingly separate no matter how much you love. I wish that I could lie down next to him, on my side, curl into him the way I used to or he into me. Maybe I would read one of those decor magazines and tell him about a new plan for the garden or a recipe I would like to try, and it would be okay if he was asleep already. It is those comforts I know he misses. The sound of turning pages. Since there are no pages to turn I sail around the house instead, looking for things I might have lost.

3

WILLIAM WAS WOKEN BY THE SOUND of the bell ringing. He took so long to open his eyes the cleaners were almost ready to get back into their van and drive to the next crime scene. He drew the curtains and greeted them from the window as cheerfully as he could.

"Give me a minute," he said, trying to smile.

The cleaners were angry-looking and he thought it was on account of the abnormal hour, when most people find it impossible to look happy. Well 7 am was the only opening they had and he wondered if the company had teams cleaning around the clock, a never-ending, bare bulb, blood-spattered life, punctuated by coffee in Styrofoam cups.

"Good morning, Mr Jenkins. We apologize for our persistent ringing but we have a schedule to keep," said the owner, the manager, the one that has asserted herself in the pecking order and gets to give the orders, and say, "You missed a spot."

William shook her hand, it felt rough and whittled away by sorrow.

"Ina Claasens," she said, in a matter-of-fact way. She introduced the others as Faadia, who had found the time to put her hair in curlers the night before, Hazel, who smiled shyly at the floor and Petra, whose face resembled a walnut shell.

He invited the women in, encumbered and burdened

as they were with the paraphernalia required to perform a miracle.

"I am sorry it looks the way it does. I mean, I haven't been in much of a state to even begin. I would rather move house if I could." William was embarrassed and he didn't know why, nobody could expect much of him at this stage anyway.

"*Ja*, no problem, we have seen much worse, right ladies?"

The ladies, dressed in maroon housecoats, all nodded their heads in a solemn manner, as if they were permanently attending funerals every place they went. Ina set the ladies to work, giving orders in a direct and polite tone.

"Some elbow grease on this chair," she directs the women. "Some tough stains on this carpet, Mr Jenkins. Do you want us to clean the mess the police left with their fingerprint kit?"

"Well, yes, clean everything you are able to. I would appreciate it."

"Right, let's get going then. Hot water ladies, as hot as you can stand it!"

William's home became a blur of soapsuds and hands scrubbing and dusting. He even helped a little, righting one shelf, finding a place for an ornament still intact. He made them coffee, apologizing for the lack of milk and something decent to eat, saying, "I haven't been out of the house really."

He found a few stale rusks at the bottom of a biscuit tin and he and the ladies dunked and ate in a strange, comforting silence. He hadn't eaten anything since his retirement party and his stomach felt raw and sensitive and prone to bouts of nausea. He wondered how he would purchase things from the supermarket from now on. What did he have to buy? There was always milk in the fridge, the cupboards had always been stocked and ready for a guest and he had never really noticed how this happened. What could his body possibly need, now that I am gone? He could live on sunlight. He had read about people like that who got tired of eating and never ate again, preferring to photosynthesize, like a hydrangea in the garden. They had said they had never felt better, able to play that round of tennis again and think with amazing focus. Low maintenance for a highly complex system? His engineering brain didn't quite believe it. They must be a new kind of crazy and that was all there was to it, in his opinion.

"You getting some help, Mr Jenkins, you know, to run the house some, cook a little?"

"I think I will be fine, just have to learn, nothing to it, right?"

He wasn't fooling Ina or himself, the word "fine", as he said it, seemed an impossible and wretched word, nothing would ever be fine again. As for the domestic business of living, he didn't even know how to boil an egg. Even the coffee had to be thought out, where was it kept, how much to use and how to work the filter machine. When he was a child, his mother had always looked after him, cutting the crusts off the bread like he liked, affectionately wiping crumbs from the corners of his mouth. Later, at university, in the various digs he found himself in, he would smear peanut butter or chocolate spread over popcorn, eat a tin of beans standing in his flip flops and dressing gown. He could just go back to that way of eating, couldn't he? He still hankered after his youth and the irresponsibility that came with it.

"I know someone who runs a little company which sends good women out to people who need a little assistance, after a tragedy or an illness. Would you like a card?"

William nodded his head without saying anything. Maybe he would call tomorrow, or next year, maybe never. He just wanted a number near, a number that offered assistance. He put the card in his pocket without looking at it. He noticed his trousers felt smooth and greasy. He wondered if he stank. He made a mental note to shower. He didn't know what to make of Ms Claasens' good intentions; he didn't know if he should feel offended or not. Of course he could look after himself; he wasn't helpless, was he? Nor was he an invalid either. He just wanted to be alone in his now sparkling house, free to shuffle from room to room, drinking till sleep came to rescue him.

Or an even lonelier thought: Ms Claasens could take him to her ample bosom and tell him it will be alright, like his mother did when he took the skin off his knees. It didn't matter much that William was older than her and she was dressed in a housecoat and menacingly brandishing a dust cloth at a chest of drawers. William wanted to sob his heart out into those warm maroon folds, find some kind of perfume on her skin that smelt like safety. He busied himself with rinsing the coffee cups and dusting the crumbs off the plates instead.

"She's a good friend of mine, trust her with my life I would. You will have no worries with her." Funny to be talking about life around here, funny to be alive at all. Yes, if I was alive I would be laughing.

"I am sorry for what happened here, Mr Jenkins. I don't know what is happening anymore to this place, gone crazy!"

"It has always been crazy, Ms Claasens."

"*Ja*, that is the truth!"

"Ever get tired of saying sorry, considering the work you do?"

"I mean it every time, if that is what you are asking," and she turned to check on her team's progress, spotting places they didn't see.

William found it hard to believe that he was having a semi normal conversation in his living room, that he found a lightness enough to open his mouth and make words come out. He didn't want it to go away, he didn't want the night to come back either, it could stay just where it was on the other side of the world.

4

You can understand, can't you, that I didn't want to be there when those women in their tidy coats came to clean up the mess I had made? I went to the park around the corner from where I lived, where William in his new loneliness carries on surrounded by the same walls.

I avoided sitting on the excuse for a lawn, littered with used condoms (I should be relieved and thankful that they are used), syringes, other unidentifiable things that result in sudden queasiness. I draped myself over the slides and swings, enjoyed an imaginary chocolate croissant, a cup of milky coffee and a cigarette.

I wondered if children ever came to play here in this little patch of Observatory. I heard a couple comment on my murder, from where I was sitting, looking over their shoulders. It looks like it made the fourth page. They were trying to will themselves away from this place with words, with ideas and plans for foreign places, where surely you don't have to fear walking in the streets. The woman played nervously with a strand of her hair and the man, a barman I knew from a pub I liked going to, shrugged his shoulders and said, "It's all shit and it's shit everywhere. The whole world has gone mad."

She refused to believe that, saying, "There must be somewhere on this godforsaken planet to go to and...

fuck, look at that story – another child murdered and raped."

She pointed angrily at the newspaper. "What is wrong with this place? Fuck, I can't stand it anymore! How do people go missing? I mean, adults I can understand, walking away from their front door, or leaving their shopping just where it is and never coming back. But children – how are they let out of anyone's sight?"

Steven the barman replied that people go missing all the time and more easily than his twitchy girlfriend thinks. "They were probably drinking, the adults that is, leaving their kids to fend for themselves, slapping them around if they come to tell them they're hungry, treat them worse than their dogs, they do. Anyone can spirit them away to a grisly and deplorable end."

"But why do they want to make grisly ends for as many as possible? That's my question!"

"It's in the history, I guess. We aren't coming from the meekest of places into a democracy. Don't you agree? Bound to be teething problems."

The conversation was getting heated and I leaned forward in my red swing, the paint peeling off, trying to hear every word in among the trucks going past.

"Teething problems!" She was really incensed now, tapping new rage, and vexed at every corner. "You call the murder and rape of an old woman and a child 'teething problems', I bet they didn't think so. I bet they thought, well, shit this isn't fair!"

Old woman? I was an old woman, I never felt that way. I had felt young, somewhere near twenty really if I think about it, always surprised at my sagging breasts and graying hair, another wrinkle and stiffness in the bones when I still wanted to leap off cliffs.

"How can you babble on about fairness in this country? We are lucky we whites weren't all shot in our beds, because if I had been in their position I would've been beyond angry that the country could just slip into a democracy with hardly a word spoken in vengeance."

"We had the Truth and Reconciliation Commission, didn't we?" she interjected between his breathing.

"You sound like one of those people who say it was all self indulgence and if I have to see one more black person wailing or hear how terrible we whites were..."

"Self indulgence? What do you mean, Steven?"

"That we should be backed into a corner if needs be, till we cover our ears with shame, who are we that we cannot hear this weeping?" Here in the sunshine of the day in this unlikely place, I swing in and out of what it means to be guilty.

"So tell me love, where did all that anger go to, where did all that trodden-upon-like-dogs go?"

Steven's partner sighed heavily and said "I don't know and I don't care, I just want to feel safe!"

"We are all in the shit together now, with no one spared from the grinning man at your window, because we all hate each other. Zulus hate Xhosas, Coloureds hate Blacks, Indians only like each other, and Whites pretend to like everyone because we are the ones that need to atone though we would never admit it. Still you don't think they talk about the *kaffirs* around their sizzling boerewors under the sunny sky they thought they owned."

"I never said we were perfect, Steven!"

"And their wives in the kitchen armed with Nathaniel cookbooks making it even prettier in the pretty suburbs, you don't think they say it to their faces, all the staff still working for the fucking white *baas*, but they put up with it because jobs are scarce. 'Those *bobbejane* and flat noses running the country into the ground.' I can fucking hear them as we speak. 'It will take a white man to make the country right again, fuck the women too, don't have the comprehension for matters of governance,' all that patriarchal shite! Whatever we have, no matter how much or how little someone will take it. We weren't ready for democracy, coming from such savagery... think we would have made the transition with a modicum of civility, well fuck civility is what I would've said!"

She made a motion to wedge a word in but he wouldn't let her.

"Yes and if the colour of your skin wasn't obvious enough, they used other measures like sticking a pencil in your hair and if it stayed stuck, well, unlucky for you, measuring the features of your face, nose and forehead, relegating you to the space that you were required to fill, the only space you could fill, though they would have done away with you all together! Those bastards making the rules that we all followed, sucked up and swallowed and you still warble on about fair!"

"Jesus Steven, I just wanted to sit a while in the sunshine, why are going on like this?"

"Because I am angry!"

She sat silent for a while, rolling up the newspaper. "Maybe, Steven, you are making excuses for an intolerable expression of behaviour, and I hate those race distinctions anyway Coloureds, Blacks, Whites, why can't we get away from it? I mean we were just kids in the time of apartheid, what were we supposed to do about it, could we do anything about it? My parents were kind of liberal, trying to make a small difference somewhere. Besides, South Africa is not much different form any other place, everywhere you go people who weren't white got a raw deal, the Aborigines in Australia, the Native Americans, kicked onto reserves, black Americans lynched and where the hell did it come from this absurd notion of superiority, starting to hate white people, hating my very own skin."

"Love, you are talking in circles. Think about it!"

Sitting on my swing I thought about it. We will never know the reasons, will we, only the symptoms? If it wasn't supported here it wouldn't have succeeded for so long, the whites should have had their own uprising, refusing to work, foiling the plans, jamming up the cogs, we could have just ceased to function till the government righted its wrongs, made it impossible for such a demeaning autocracy to continue and flourish, but why when we were privileged, when we were comfy in our homes and we could walk into jobs straight off the street and we could go anywhere in our white skins. That is the thing about humanity, I don't believe in its innate goodness, as we in South Africa were happy to prosper while the other half was forced to disappear from basic dignity. No, we will have to ride this one out, till we can find our way out of the septic tank of our history.

Would they agree with me if they could hear me that it all smells worse if you come up close or the wind is just right. She folded her arms around herself and said in his direction that her mother was expecting her for a visit but she would be back later, maybe they could go out for dinner, watch a movie with a bowl of popcorn between them?

"Yeah, sure," he said and she bent to kiss his head.

"You take it all to heart, Steven, get so twisted up about it."

"How else am I supposed to take it?"

She gave him a worn down smile, walked down the street with the newspaper under her arm. Watching him light a cigarette and putting the soft pack back in his jean pocket, I remembered the gin and tonic he used to serve me, how he would try and coax me to have an outlandish cocktail, something brazen and colourful like a lounge singer who smoked too much and always got laid: "Go on Sarah, this will put some hair on your chest; life is too short anyway!" So it was.

He stood up from the bench, stretched his arms a little and looked before crossing the street, waving hello to faces he knew.

I took another way home, down a more elegant-looking street. The grand old Victorian ladies with their brookie-laced verandas and parochial windows. Not all of our pedagogy was ugly, was it?

I passed two women kissing and thought love is near if you care to find it, look for it: an instance of tenderness in unlikely times. I knew Imogen had women lovers as well as men. Colour was never an issue with her either. Not that I had any problem with it. What problem could there be with love? Imogen assumed that I would disapprove and came brandishing an argument all filed in her head.

"I know your religion frowns upon this, but you think you have some biblical authority on love – that there is only heterosexual missionary style love around and that your love is the only love allowed and permitted any freedom and acknowledgment?"

She hardly stopped for breath and I interrupted her, saying I wasn't all that religious and even if I was it wouldn't make any difference to me if she brought a Martian home with a flatulence problem, as long as she was happy! She seemed perplexed at the mention of the word "happy", even stopped talking for a minute.

"Who is happy, Mother? Who has that little luxury of being happy? Such a trite word! A terrible insolent arrogance happiness is. I spit on it. How can I be happy when I know somebody else isn't?"

I lost the meaning of happiness against those long ago thorn trees and knew its meaning would never come back – that I would always live around the word, glance at it, bemused and wholly distrustful.

"Every man, woman and child for themselves, Imogen. You can't go carry the world in your head."

"You're such a capitalist, Mother, letting somebody fall through the cracks because they didn't know how to make twenty bucks out of ten."

"You can't judge me for having lived in no other system!"

"There, you said it Ma: *system*. And the system will say it is in our nature to better ourselves, to want more and to want that semi at the sea and to struggle and sweat for it. But that system makes up the rules of what that struggle is and keeps most of the population in servitude to those who made it to that bloody semi at the sea. And they only made it there because they knew somebody who knew somebody."

"Imogen, not everyone can be wealthy, someone has to keep the mundane going, the factories turning, not true?"

"It's what the system wants you to believe – that you can't make money without pissing on another person's dreams, without exploiting another!"

As she went on relentlessly I noticed my temples developing a subtle throb. Of course, she was right. There is only one life to live. I don't think any person would want to waste it at the hands of another, compromise what they wanted again and again.

"Well, fuck, I am here, born into this system and powerless against it. What do you want me to do, Imogen, stop dreaming and stop wanting?"

She was surprised I had used the F-word, and she wondered how to continue, if she should continue at all.

"It's all fucked up, Mother, and I wish it wasn't, that is all."

"I know, dear." I smoothed a crease in the tablecloth and offered her another coconut cookie.

I noticed her car in the road, parked outside our gate. She was still sitting in it with her head on the steering wheel, wondering if she should turn around and go missing. William opened the door for her and I slipped in, pleased to see that he'd had a shower and changed his clothes. A threadbare tracksuit hung from his frame. The house bore hardly any marks from the incident, only some of the things thrown around still lying about, some haphazardly pushed to corners to clear a walk way. The cleaners had done a brilliant job and I wish I could have thanked them.

Imogen kissed her father on the cheek and handed

him a parcel.

"Thought you might need these," she said to him in a distracted manner, not sure how to meet his eyes.

Looking like a little boy he peered into the packet, his back slightly stooped, the morning sun from the open door soft on his face. In the packet were milk, a packet of chocolate chip cookies, a square TV dinner for one. Something tasteless and stodgy, I am sure. Oh Imogen, could you not have done a little better. He is your father. Consider what he is going through! I would've whacked her on the head if I had had the hands to do so. Did I teach you nothing, my daughter?

She had sat herself down on the couch, brushed strands of hair from her face, crossed her legs and waited for her father to shuffle in from the passage.

"Ah, thank you, dear. I was just meaning to go out and get milk."

"Well, the least I could do, you know, considering." Imogen could never tell when her father was entertaining sarcasm.

He put the packet on the kitchen counter, taking the milk and the dinner for one to the fridge. That left just the cookies in the now capacious plastic packet. He would save them for a guest, there would be many of those soon, in and out, and during the funeral, and then they would stay away thinking the grief must be over. Their attentions will be reduced to just the occasional phone call. William sighed at the thought of the energy it would take to arrange the funeral, to put on a stoic face. Maybe Imogen could be of some help, pedantic and practical as she was. She could help him give her mother a befitting goodbye, though he would rather keep her inside as he remembers her. What business did anyone else have with the way he loved her; it had nothing to do with them.

"Would you like some coffee, your old dad managed to brew a pot this morning for the cleaners, fancy that!"

"Yes, fancy that indeed. I would like a cup, thank you." The meeting wasn't going very well, I could see. They were stuttering and stammering all over the place, too polite. William busied himself with finding the filter paper, measuring two heaped spoons of Columbia's finest, talking as he watched the coffee drip drip into the glass pot.

"Lovely people," he said, for lack of a better thing to say.

"Who?"

"The cleaners. Run a tight ship they do, no job too big for them or disgusting, or sad really, if you think of it."

Imogen smiled uncomfortably at her father.

"You have your mother's smile, Imogen." William's legs felt heavy as if they were shod in irons, his gut hollow with a wrenching sense of irretrievable loss.

"Is that a good or a bad thing, Dad?"

"A good thing, I would like to think."

I remember how William was when Imogen was born. He loved her from first sight, was crazy about her, and she could do no real wrong in his eyes and she was a real daddy's girl, clambering onto his back when he came home, kissing his cheeks.

I was clinical and distant, changing her nappies as required, breastfeeding her, rocking her a little when she cried, but it was always William who managed to lull her to sleep. From the very beginning we were at odds with each other, though I loved her more than anything or anyone and I could imagine killing anyone who harmed her.

How did it end up like this between them, then? All that distance made me feel sorry for William, as he drank his coffee and wondered what to say. It had been easy once.

"Where did it happen, Dad? I mean where did you find Mom?"

"You are looking at it. In her chair. It didn't look like this though." William stopped where he was going, thinking it unnecessary to tell his daughter the awful details.

"Here, right here in front of where I am?"

"Yes, sweetheart."

I could see she didn't know what to feel, or how to feel it; she wasn't one for crying, rather letting everything stew and fester inside of her. I envied her control.

"I don't know what to say, Dad, how to even begin to feel it, all of it is utter madness, I can't even believe it yet. When you told me I thought you were lying, playing some sick prank on me. And I still think Ma is going to come out of the bedroom and shout, "Surprise!"

"Imogen don't..."

"Don't? What do you mean 'don't'? Sorry if I don't know how to behave when my mother gets murdered! Who were they, how the hell did they get in, how in fuck did it happen, where were you Dad, where were you?"

William hung his head as far into his track top as it would go. He looked exhausted and cupped the mug of coffee with both hands.

"I was at work. A stupid retirement goodbye cheese and wine, I dropped in on my own retirement party. Your mother and I were going to go out afterwards." He was mumbling, feeling like it was all his fault, that he hadn't been the gallant knight wielding a baseball bat.

Imogen began crying somewhere in the middle of his answer. She made a pitiful wailing sound and William went to hold her in his arms. He couldn't let his own tears go, wanting to hold onto them, afraid of what they would look like once free, afraid of what they would sound like, when he finally realized that I was dead.

Imogen didn't cry for long and she pulled away from him, rubbed her reddened face angrily, tapped the heel of her boot to some rhythm she had in her head. William offered her a tissue and she blew her nose noisily, crumpled it up into a soggy ball, held it in her hand, too stricken to get up and throw it away.

Somewhere in the devastation that overwhelmed Imogen, she grasped the practical and held on to it as if it was a strong arm over a precipice she was looking into, a normal arrangement in the encroaching chaos and abject sorrow. She could be strong for her father, couldn't she? Get herself busy and her mind way clear of feeling anything.

"The funeral, Dad, has anything been arranged?"

William brushed a piece of blue thread from his pants and said that he couldn't comprehend the invitations, the phone calls, not knowing what to say. Not knowing what flowers I would've liked.

"I can help, Dad. I mean, leave it to me. I don't think it is something you should have to do single-handedly, or do at all, it is too much for you now."

"Too much for both of us Imogen. It is an impossible thing, diabolical, and when I find those people... when I find them..." His voice trailed away and Imogen said I would have liked St Joseph's lilies, and that I wouldn't want it to be sad. Well, she was right with the choice of flowers, but I think I would want some tears to be shed as it wasn't meant to be this way, this wasn't right. Had I been 90 and toothless I wouldn't want a single person standing, would've wanted everyone drunk and playing cards, smoking cigars and the music loud and old couples still getting laid in the garden. I can't imagine any mourners at this funeral at all. I imagine something so quiet, so terribly still, where words and voices fail and no one would know how to pay their respects. Would they even eat the funeral sandwiches and square slices of cake?

I left them to their burial plans, with their words lying like lead butterflies in my missing solar plexus, turning histories loose with each beating wing. I need to find my stories, the short ones that I had stacked neatly in alphabetical order before all hell came to visit me in my home. I want to turn the pages over in my hands, run my fingers over familiar, treacherous places. I know if I lie still and quiet enough, I could make sense of them, move them and put to rights the mess they made. The mess they have always bloody made.

5

A STORY IS A WORD DRAWN OUT.

I have nightmares. Do you believe me? Who ever heard
of a dead person having nightmares? I assume it is
post-traumatic stress. I cry from eyes I can't touch, I
jump at shadows and sudden movements; the night is
close and sinister around my throat because I cannot
sleep, because I cannot leave and I don't want to think
anymore. I find no relief from the images that plague
me and this is my story, written in a minor key. Rescue
me from this night, touch and soothe my brow, stop
the shaking, the foreboding sky scarred with wagon
wheels and *volkspele* and the *predikant* lying through
his false teeth about love and tolerance on Sundays.
The *Dromedaris*, sailing ghostlike through my head
and the white hand that touched the black soil and
fucked it, red coats and shiny brass buttons, having
their way against assegais, burning kraals and oiled
black skins. We are all savages fucking what we want,
killing what we don't like, we are all on fire, in the back
rooms where no one is watching, in bars, on our way
to work. We walk over and over into insignificance,
the footsteps of those who brought us here.

The top of my head is going to blow off, I know
this, and crows fluid and dark are going to touch
the tips of the sky. Vultures will eventually come to

68

peck at my eyes. This is a wretched curse cast from love, a separateness that turns in my hands, round and complete like a glass bead, roll it away, let it go. It is only a circle that knows no escape from itself, a circle that lives in the irises of my eyes, eternally unknowing of the possibility of light. My homily, my thousand words and thousand tears for every little face frightened in the night. The little girl in the papers like me, and her eyes wide with terror, found her in a drain they did, along with the filth and stink that lives there, truth closed around her like a fist, her mouth bound in question marks and the hot breath of terror. Speak to me, world. You pretend to care and march and march and march.

I am bigger than most girls I have come across in this place, yes, bigger than you can imagine, even with this hole in my heart. You could say I am a giantess, awkward and out of proportion, my mouth that likes the silence is huge and cavernous and ignorant in my nondescript face. I could be anyone, the girl next door. I could live any way I choose if it wasn't for my size.

Mother likes to paint my face in order to attract the customers, to make me look like a caricature of innocence, a sweetness that is only horrifying to me, the way clowns are known to scare very small children. I stride from one star to the next and tell her it is always sore, she sweeps my words under my ribs where they go to die. I never chose this. Who would?

I have siren red lips, little brown freckles that Mother dabs onto my cheeks with angered detachment. "No one could resist you," she says. She paints and makes me pretty just to turn it around for it is always us who wanted it, the ones who seduced and lured our innocence into leaving, who ever believes us, for we are always the liars aren't we? I am not ever sure why it is this way, like the circle in my eyes that can never escape from the misfortune of being born a girl.

I wear a kiss-me-quick dress, fashioned after the illustrations of *Alice in Wonderland*, elaborate frills – anything can get lost in them, even myself. My feet are clad in black-buckled shoes, white lace socks find their way to the middle of my calf. My outfit is specially made, seeing that I am the size I am. Mother expends a lot of energy into her thoughtlessness, and there are tailors all over town, all over this dark wretched scenery that are happy to agree with her and entertain her. They sit at their sewing machines, with their fat sausage fingers and ham hands growing red-painted nails. The smell of unwashed women and stale musk, a jingling bangle keeping time with the second hand in the oily night. So the women sew me in and sew me up, stitch by intricate stitch and in the night when I become an inch too much, and too small where there is no place else to fly to, the women take me in and tell me to stop fussing, telling me the moon looks the same, though I am crying blood.

I am chained to a pole most nights. A bright maypole, cemented into the ground, rainbow after rainbow in the observers' eyes, from a distance I could be laughing. There is no gypsy van or room in a fixed domicile large enough for my frame. I hear the animals keen for something to remember. The animals are in their filthy stinking cages and have no soft place to lie. No respite from the wounds inflicted from the previous performances, the whipping, the tricks, the stand-up-

and-beg routines, elephants standing and toppling over one another while the crowd laughs, their trainer driving them hard with white teeth in a thankless grimace. What does the trainer know of places that die, places that run with sweat and misery in the middle of the night, the beginning of the morning wide-eyed and sickened to the stomach. No, I don't want to eat anymore, want to make myself smaller, invisible so I can disappear.

Mother says I should be grateful for the gift I have been given, and she throws a peanut in my mouth that I catch perfectly between my milk teeth. Yes, there are sadder things right in front of me. The woman who weighs 400 kilograms is sadder than I am. She lives in a glass house and everyone guffaws and gasps at her, or laughs outright and insults her and points their fingers. She sits on a little velvet chair, especially reinforced to carry her awesome size. Of course, it took a master crafter to make the size of woman to say he could make the chair that didn't break under her, like my dresses and the tailors in the night, because when we don't fit into the image they made, it is always our fault then.

The audience feed her cream cakes through a tiny slit, and she never disappoints them, always finishing every crumb that is offered. Licking her fingers victoriously; her teeth and her capacity outdoing each and every expectation. There is always a crowd around her, sometimes I think she is the only reason anyone ever visits the circus, she is what the circus owner would call a stellar attraction and the circus would surely fall to its knees and cease to exist without her and the men and women who perpetuate her demise.

After the spectacle is over, after all her bravery and

courage has run from her, she sinks into that little velvet chair, her immense mountainous arms slack and lifeless at her sides, I hear her weeping and choking on her crumbs. Her eyes after the rain staring at an iced rose which she neglected to eat.

Laugh while they can, we all say; the removal of our dead bodies will be a spectacle too, ringside seats and the popcorn will be on special. We know how to grow hard and bitter as gall.

Bile in my smile as the men come one after the other, getting lost in my frills and taking a peek up my dress. Mother opens her hand and they toss coins for a more thorough look at the freak. They clamber up my legs, between my legs, like vines with thorns, and how far up will I have to go to not feel them anymore, till they become smaller than me? The wives pass time with their kids shooting plastic ducks for a prize and become irritable, as they walk around and around the circus grounds. They return to look for their men stuck in my dress. "If you don't come out now I am coming in to fetch you," they say, stabbing lemon popsicles in and out of their pert little mouths. They clip their sons on the ear as they try for a sneak view of their first girl. The mothers smile as they halfheartedly chastise accepted rites. Do I have any such rites or am I only ever losing my virginity? Losing the skin from the hole, where all hell finds its way in?

Yes, if I ever come back to such a place, it would be as a trapeze artist, soaring and flying and hands that catch me and never let me fall. I would have feathers and sequins in my hair and instead of gasps of revulsion I would hear sighs of adoration and wonderment and the sound of anxious silence before I fly through the air.

I could set myself on fire. There are artists here who have a way with fire. Flames from their mouths fly in umber-coloured arches wowing the eyes of the onlookers, making their eyes dance. I could do it, where would I start, at my feet, or the top of my head? Would it hurt so much that I would know I had made a mistake? Doing this just to make the pain stop? Inch by inch the fire would consume me. Afterwards, when it is all over, and I am no longer here you can show my ribbons to your friends. Or now that your eyes have finally been opened, would you begin to cry?

I think of Venus, the Hottentot Venus. I think of a country that cannot think itself beyond its fevered landscape and convenient memory. She was brought back in pieces instead, some consolation and so we wonder what is any different deep on the inside, deep in the rhythm of what makes our songs desolate and treacherous, the way we sing to each other, turning in our pain, our collective nightmares we are too afraid to really touch, to admit. Our misogynist history, firmly rooted in strata upon strata of injustice leaves me wondering why no one can smell our anger. But she had pendulous, fantastic labia we couldn't refuse. Buttocks you could find shade under and breasts that hung low and exposed. A freak in the European context, a sideshow, a roadside attraction, a fascination milked and exploited to barbaric ends. Chained to a pole for the delight or horror of the passers by. Look! Look at what we found in Africa! Was she found in the diaries of the colonizers next to the drawings of the animals and birds they found there, catalogued and defined? And did her own treat her any better?

6

THE SILENCE IS UNBEARABLE IN THE HOUSE, William is as invisible as I am but I have found meaning enough to hold my pages, to leaf through the words that I had written, and he has found his way to my hermitage, thumbing things I used to own. He has a perplexed look on his face, wondering why the room is ordered and everything in its place. The hairs rise on his arms and he folds them across his chest. I see no reason why he should be afraid of me, his good wife who always made sure he was fed and twisted the bedsheets with her limbs as he learned how to love her. He rubs his eyes against the perpetual need to crawl into bed and never get up again. Oh, I know, William, I know how you feel. Why we bother with anything at all is a mystery to me.

He glances back to where I am standing, maybe he thinks he sees me, or glimpses a shadow, a spot in his peripheral vision. But I know he doesn't. He closes the door behind him and I can hear him make his slow sad way down the stairs.

Imogen is keeping herself busy with my funeral arrangements, finding and phoning people even I had forgotten about. Really, darling, is this necessary? I hardly knew these people, I know you want the world to know but I would rather have no funeral at all. Can't you see that? She carries on punching in the numbers,

74

holding her breath to tell the news. She phoned her grandmother first, but grandmother already knew, telling her that mothers know. "We have eyes in the backs of our heads," she said. She had been so upset by her premonition that she climbed into a bottle of vodka and then another. Two nights blind drunk cursing her dead husband and the phantom bruises when she touched her cheeks because they still stung, cursing my senseless death. Curling herself up into a foetal position, biting her knuckles in time with the spasms in her chest, realizing for once and for all that life was a rotten business and that the light in her eyes would go out all at once, of that she was sure.

"My womb hurts, Imogen. A mother should never lose a child. It touches something that will never heal. The slimy bastards, if I lay my hands on them, hang 'em in the streets I will!" Grandmother howled and blubbered into the phone and I could only feel a familiar annoyance, like, get up, Mother, stop lying there like it happened to you, let me have my day, it isn't about you! Imogen unable to deal with her sobbing grandmother said that the doorbell was ringing and she had to go. She put the phone down before her grandmother could work herself into renewed bouts of crying right through Imogen's ear, straight down where the loss of me turned her guts into writhing coils.

From this distance, I can get a bird's eye view of my life, and I find I didn't have that many close friends. Anyway, friends get busy with husbands or wives, busy with children and we always meant to keep up some of the wild old ways; the parties where tired potbellied cops answered to the neighbours' calls that the Jenkinses were disturbing the peace again. When something really momentous happens, nobody calls, nobody hears a damn thing! So it comes to a handful of numbers that will find out that I am dead. What a sorry, shitty story, and I want no part of it.

Imogen went to fetch the *Yellow Pages*, lugging its bulk in both hands and dumping it on her cluttered desk. She ran her finger down the list of florists, eventually speaking with a woman who managed to convince her that a splash of colour wouldn't do any harm. "How about some blood orange roses dear, mixed in with touches of green, I think that would look just beautiful, funerals don't need to be, you know, monochromatic anymore."

Imogen doesn't know, she wants to put the phone down in the annoying woman's ear. How dare she tell her what would look beautiful, considering the circumstances, her mother was dead and she was going on about hues and tonality! What she really wanted to ask was why, why was she burying her mother so soon! She didn't even have the time to get around to the grandchildren. She meant to, sometime, someday, she would move into the suburbs and find a husband named Bob who mowed the lawn on Saturdays. Imogen, you couldn't imagine anything worse could you, don't go beating yourself up, I was never much of a mother, wouldn't have been the best grandmother, maybe it's better this way. And why don't you have any friends that can arrange flowers? You could ask Emily, my closest friend, she took the same course I did, but she actually finished it, even advertised herself, you should phone her, she would want to know. I wish you could hear me!

Imogen tells the woman the colour is to be

understated: "Nothing gaudy please."

They are in agreement and Imogen puts the phone down, muttering something unfriendly under her breath.

She speaks to a priest from a Catholic church I used to attend (yes, I know, but it isn't my fault my father was Catholic). He apologizes for her loss in sanctimonious tones, "The Lord works in mysterious ways and we are called when we are needed." So far I haven't been needed for anything, been mucking about in limbo watching the people I love handle my death, talking to a dead man on a taxi.

She phones a caterer, funeral food is not the same as it once was either and Imogen is bombarded with questions. Would you like dips? What kind of theme are you aiming for? Tuscan luncheon, salads drizzled with balsamic vinegar? A set sit-down menu, finger snacks?

"Whatever happened to the good old sausage rolls and the cucumber sandwiches that someone's aunt made?" Imogen asked.

There was silence on the other side.

"Finger snacks then, that will be fine." She couldn't imagine anyone wanting to linger around long enough to ingest a whole sit-down meal. Neither could I. I would make excuses, like that I had left Jimmy with a babysitter I couldn't really trust or my infirm grandmother needs to be turned in her bed.

Imogen drove back to her father's home with lists in her head and news to tell. William was eating a bowl of instant oats. Just add hot water. Strawberry-flavoured. Telling Imogen that it's the only thing that sits well with him. Strange expression that, as opposed to something that lunges you in the ribs or gets itchy, starts becoming difficult and demanding.

"That isn't really food, Dad."

"Well I know, but what does it matter?"

"You should keep your strength up."

William ignored her, not seeing the point of keeping anything up, especially his frame.

"I sorted the flowers, the priest, the food and phoned just about everyone Mother ever knew."

"You spoke to your grandmother?"

"Yes, tells me she already knew. She sounded drunk."

"She knows because I told her the next morning or day, I can't remember a damn thing anymore."

"Funny that. She said nobody told her. Said she knew it deep down in her belly."

"Such a drama queen Angela is, did you get hold of Emily?"

William put his half eaten bowl of oats on the kitchen counter and wipes his mouth with the clean end of a dishtowel.

"Who is Emily?"

"One of your mother's closest and dearest, we can't forget about her. I'll phone her now." William had to look through all my old telephone books to find her number. She had moved from the apartment she had lived in for ten years. The present tenant had a forwarding number. She had moved to some artists' haven in Calitzdorp where the property was still attainable, and I imagined her home, splinters of mirror and blue glass in the stucco walls and tomato plants in rusted coffee and bean tins. Soft light in every room no matter the heat or the angle of the sun.

I hadn't spoken to her in years and I was almost envious that William could speak to her, catch up on all the news if he was interested. It made me realize how much I had missed her. That's the uncomfortable thing about death, realizing too many things that you have no hope of ever changing now.

Once William had got past the pleasantries of the mundane questions, like *how are you?*, and told her the news, she became quiet. Maybe she was thinking of something, remembering something that only we ever knew about, ever shared, and the indigo clouds in the grey twilight from a window in a room we never went back to. I can see it now, filling my eyes with a light I had never seen before.

"She would want you to be there, Emily." William shifted from his left foot to his right. He always did that when he was uncomfortable or didn't know what to say.

"Yes, of course I will be there."

William said goodbye in a barely audible voice, took another spoonful of now cold and stodgy oats, put the spoon down, disgusted and nauseated. "You are right Imogen, this isn't real food."

"Sounds like there is some kind of history with Emily, Dad."

"Your mother's business dear. Respect the sanctity of her privacy."

I was surprised he didn't say anything, the dead are only dead, what would they care about airing the laundry to those still alive?

"Okay, Dad. Whatever you say."

"Yes, and I will say no more about it, understand?"

He was still angry, then, bitter and twisted, however abiding and tolerant he might have been back then.

Imogen's ears were burning with curiosity but she nodded her head, maybe he would tell her some day, years from now if they were still around.

"Well, I have to go, have an article to write, though I don't know why I bother when nothing can be helped."

"I don't know how you can even think of writing at this time. Why are we all going on as if this is normal? My wife is dead, raped and murdered, and you are worrying about some bloody article you have to write. God, you are selfish, always have been!" William found that bowl of oats and flung it at the nearest empty wall. It broke unsatisfactorily into three pieces with a muffled clunk.

William seemed crazed. He leaned on the counter with his elbows.

"Shit fuck fuck fuck, God I can't do it, I can't bear another second without her, I want to die Imogen, why wasn't it me instead, old useless buzzard, why wasn't it me, I can't anymore, pretend that it will be okay." Before my husband could stop it, tears ran from his eyes, blinding him, turning his startled daughter into a watermark. He slid down to the floor, on his knees as if he was praying at an altar, his mouth open in a silent howl that found sound as he breathed and gasped for air.

Neither Imogen nor I had ever heard a scream from William. Travelling lonely as it did from the dark pit of his stomach, deep and agonized, his tears unchecked and choking in his throat. I could hardly watch, yet I was transfixed, rooted to the spot by how absolutely naked and beautiful he looked and how hideous all at once. I couldn't help him, couldn't rock him in my arms and tell him there wasn't a minute that I didn't miss him, long for him and that I was lonely too.

Imogen, not knowing what to do with her broken and beaten father, went to sit near him, touching his wet hands. His cry had slowed down to a soft whimpering. She stroked his knuckles, felt the soft brown hairs beneath her fingers, how vulnerable he was, how vulnerable we all are she thought.

William must have cried for an hour with Imogen sitting silently next to him, rubbing his trembling hands. I sat on his other side, leaning into him and tried the best I could to hold him up.

When William managed to rise from his feet I could have sworn he had aged twenty years before my eyes. He looked dead and only his dumb machine heart kept on beating because it didn't know any better.

"I'm sorry, sweetheart, I didn't mean what I said earlier; you know, about you being selfish. I was angry."

"It's okay, probably the truth anyway, no hard feelings."

Imogen made him a cup of tea which he sipped slowly, seemingly in a trance, staring at the geraniums through the window.

"Could you water the garden please? It must be like a desert out there, I haven't got to it yet."

"Sure, Dad."

Outside, Imogen wrestled with the hose and cursed the knots. She wiped her eyes with the back of her hand. The garden looked relieved though; I could almost hear the roots drinking and sucking, petals beginning to turn outwards again and leaves lifting from their wilted dispositions. I sat on the steps, like I used to, watching my daughter take care of my garden in my absence. How beautiful she has become, I never really noticed it before, never really looked at her. It was easy to fall in love with her, impossible to live with her, what with the world she carried in her head, not much space for good cheer. I wish she would smile more, relax her shoulders and – God! – believe she deserved some kind of happiness or contentment at least.

I touched a strand of her hair, kissed her on her cheek and I wondered if she knew that I tended the garden with her.

She put her father to bed. The crying had exhausted him, taken everything out of him. She gently took off his shoes, easing his knobbly legs underneath the musty covers.

"I am so tired. Never felt so tired in all my life."

"I know, Dad, I know."

"Thank you for your kindness, dear."

She put her slender index finger to her lips, hushing him.

He rolled onto his side and fell asleep before he could find a comfortable position for his head. She kissed him on his clammy forehead and closed the door behind her.

7

I FOLLOWED HER HOME, wanting to be with her, talk with her, missing our heated conversations, or just to look at her, so I could remember every feature, every line of her face, every idiosyncrasy of movement. What would she do if she knew her dead mother was in the passenger seat, telling her to slow down and watch out for that woman with her pram, pressing the imaginary brake through the floor? Scream, fall into a dead faint or ramp the sidewalk?

The drive home annoyed her and she swore at the taxi drivers changing lanes without warning, cutting in front of her, jumping red robots. She baled out of her car as if there was an emergency, running up her steps, fumbling for her keys and felt the relief of the open door and the silence. She walked straight to her fridge and poured herself a drink – vodka like her grandmother.

"Can't smell it on you, wonderful stuff," she would tell Imogen, who was listening intently at her grandmother's knee.

She sifted through her post, leaving the accounts unopened. There was a postcard from a friend studying in London; everything was "just fabulous there, daahrling!"

She drained the first glass in one thirsty, desperate gulp and poured another, taking the bottle and her glass to her study. I found a place to sit on her threadbare corduroy couch. It was near the window and a weak winter sun made the room seem more cheerful and warm.

She turned on her laptop and stared at the blank screen, taking sips between thoughts that wouldn't turn into words.

Go on, you can say something; I've never known you to be lost for words! I got up, rubbed her shoulders that felt tense and knotted. She rolled her neck from left to right till she heard it click.

That isn't very good for you. Give you problems later it will. She did the same with her knuckles, click click click.

She began to type: *The Pedagogy of Gender.*

I have never had much time for people who read over other people's shoulders, but since I am dead I don't think she will notice. Pedagogy; I had to think or remember what the word meant first: teaching, education. Someone with a whip telling you how it is here on this dusty planet. Imogen's fingers remained poised over the keyboard, waiting for words that came a sentence at a time, marked with long pauses. She stared out of the window.

Gender divisions continue to mar the very freedoms that are enshrined in our constitution.

They do? What kind of a statement is that? It's dead in the water before you have even started, point counter point! Don't you know it is all just words on paper and means nothing in particular in the real world? What freedoms, Imogen? Women still smile sheepishly in adverts and wash the dirty clothes. Women are still not allowed to say "no". And what about the divisions that exist between men, people who have and don't have? Is it about gender at all?

She continues to type with a marked lack of interest.

South Africa is not defined as an area experiencing internal civil conflict yet it "boasts" the highest rape and sexual violence statistics. As these are reported incidences the number is much higher in reality. Are we proud of this accolade? Do we wear it like a badge for the world to see?

Are the people are entirely immobilized in learned helplessness? The government, complacent and lack-adaisical in forming any clear and practical solution to the intensifying and ever-increasing barbarism of the crimes committed, refuses to acknowledge that the situation is spiralling out of control.

Yes, we are experiencing an internal civil conflict though it is not defined as such, or made official. I know what you mean to say, but who is listening? How many people must be murdered, fucked and shot before the government classifies it as war?

The sun and the shade make sweeping statements across my daughter's face.

The ruling party's apathy can be reasoned into explanations that allow it to excuse itself in the broader historical context. The experienced social and moral decay is not apartheid, therefore it cannot be seen to cause fear or shame.

85

Yes, Imogen, we should all be happy and relieved that we were saved and rescued from that wretched dictatorship. Anything but that dictatorship is allowed then? We can slacken the reigns, let go of them even! We can excuse anything that fills and takes its place. Yet that anything else carries on the legacy of violence and disregard. Why would a word like "democracy" change how people behave towards each other, how would moving from one system to the next dissipate the innate rage that has always resided in this country?

Men who only ever had something to fight for, emasculated and dehumanized by white men, created their own codes, their own pecking orders of power and mostly at the expense of women.

Imogen, do you think it's only men who aren't white who treat women like crap? What about your grandfather, breaking just about every bone in your grandmother's body? What about my Uncle Bruce? What about those thick-necked ones waiting for their meals at the table, never letting their wives do anything or have an opinion. What about honour killings? It isn't only in South Africa, misogyny is everywhere, either in overt or subtle ways but, dear God, it is always there. Do you think I could ever open my mouth and speak from myself, without being the wife or the mother or the porn bitch, or cut and quartered how men think we should be, always only ever how men see us and define us under their thumbs? What would I say, Imogen, what would all of us say? It would be so loud it would burst our brains, shred the skin from our bones if we spoke from ourselves and not for ourselves. Yes, if I could cut the words from my

throat, that is how they would sound. Don't tell me your
mother doesn't understand the weight of this world.

Why do we never think that we fuck the man and
not the usual way around? We receive the man, make
space for him, let him know that he needs to know
how to treat us if he is going to get anywhere. Nothing
much we can do with a limp dick, now is there? I don't
feel respected here, I am sure no one does, this is a life
raped to the hilt and how dare we complain?

*Culture and religion can pardon any atrocity. They
can even make atrocity seem befitting to a community.
Culture then, can be entirely injurious when it refuses
to accommodate current paradigms, ignoring all signs
that certain practices undermine existence.*

Tell me, Imogen, what would the Cape Flats be without
their pseudo rap "American" gangs shooting up the
place with their pants hanging down, killing you for
their next "Tik" fix?

*The machismo is obvious and girls and women are
often raped to prove that the gang member is man
enough, the physical power he wields against women
asserts his power in the gang's ranks, promotes him in
a setting that has lost its sense of dignity, as there is no
access to any semblance of normality.*

Well of course and why not, in a backdrop of
discouraging and desperate poverty, in such a place
violence seems to be the only means to an end, doesn't
it, gangs that live on the edges and become laws unto
themselves?

Many women fall pregnant in an attempt to receive the paltry child grant, their poverty so desperate that they reason that a little over R100 a month outweighs the actual enormous monetary costs of raising a child. Men loathe to wear condoms give their partners no choice but to fall pregnant.

How many times does the government have to beg and plead that safe and preventive sex is practiced? Is that what you meant to say? I thought we would be getting the message now.

Freedom of choice should never be negated. There needs to be a clear and practical correspondence to the democratic rights enshrined in our constitution. Presently, what is written on paper means little in reality.

In the public domain sexual behaviour that is permissible for men and sexual behaviour that is permissible for women are often in conflict. What is a gendered rite of passage for one, mostly undermines the sexual autonomy of another. Men appear to have a monopoly in deciding their own natural order by naturalizing rape and negating choice in a democracy that wishes the contrary.

How terribly and persistently cruel it all is! Are we not obliged to honour what has been written on paper, this wish list that feels like a one day or some day?

Why has South Africa not internalized the constitution as its moral compass? We seem hell bent on digging our own graves, sitting in our own muck waiting for wishes to materialize. What we do and what we decide affects the whole doesn't it? Shouldn't we start thinking holistically as a country? Who we hurt today someone else will feel it tomorrow.

It seems all are ensconced in self-defining practices that are mirrored in the realm of public observation. The observed behaviour reflects that the lives of others are put in jeopardy in favour of following what the definition of self dictates.

I wish you could tell me the truth, Imogen. I often passed the places you speak of, and imagined the neat and impeccably clean homes. I imagined a crocheted tablecloth underneath the tea things and the smell of floor polish. A mother worried to the quick of her nails, ironing her son's shirt, not knowing where he is. A mangy scabby dog tied to the railing of a staircase, a flower box on a balcony, laundry strung between the dismal blocks of flats. How can anyone live here, is anyone expected to live here? How do those norms you speak of change, how many people have to drop like flies from Aids before he puts on a condom, before she can feel safe enough to refuse sex without it?

Behind the walls, behind the smoke and the drunken haze, behind skirts that are lifted and buttons undone, how does the story go? We know it well, at dreary socials in the suburbs, the boy and the girl up against a wall, in the parents' car. "It's only his dick," she says. "Can't get pregnant from oral sex... duh, like hey man." In the shack, thinking there is a bare fuck without consequence, you know she doesn't really want to, but then there is that money she can get, but what about HIV? "Hey, don't worry, baby; it's all a lie.

Come, you can't refuse me." The schoolgirl meeting the teacher because he gives her money for the ride back home, something to eat, or nothing at all, just because he wants to. The schoolboys corner her because they can, because it is their right. Why did she bother going to school, why did she bother dreaming, of getting out or getting anywhere, opening her pages for the next lesson, if it meant this, this that she knows so well? Why did her mother bother walking the streets, up and down looking for a job she never gets to afford those books, that new uniform? "Yes, our daughter will make it right, make us proud." Somewhere else, someone pinned under the savage chest of the night fighting to get free.

Isn't it getting boring yet? Imogen aren't you bored yet with all these words that will never change anything. Nothing is mighty anymore, neither the word nor the sword. It is only ever sad. You may as well tell us that you understand what leaves on trees are saying to each other, because life isn't getting any better.

The sound of Imogen's fingers falling through hollow words, her eyes I know are tired.

What could sexual freedom and sexual equality mean when cultures don't allow for these concepts or even value them? How would it be practised in South Africa, or at the very least, be taken cognizance of, when in the individual's structured socialization contrary behaviours are encouraged and the extremes of gender disparity and expressed violence are normalized.

You make it sound like we are just coming around to our natures, that the present is a new thing and we are all suddenly shocked, as though any of it dares to happen. My great grandmother survived the British concentration camps in the Boer war. Did you know that? Well I can't blame you for not knowing, I never told you and she wouldn't go telling me, a four-year-old, about such alien miseries. She breathed her last two days before I turned five and took most of her ghosts with her. My grandmother told me a few of the details while nursing her herbal bitters before bed.

"You come from a strong people, Sarah," she said to me.

"Strong as an ox my mother was, even when they took her away to those ghastly camps. She wasn't even twenty. The British army thought they could wear down the resolve of the Boer men by capturing the women and children and killing them. The army underestimated them, or maybe they were so caught up in their own causes it wouldn't have made a difference anyway. Women, we have our own history."

This would always come out if I wanted a new dress, or if I had to wring a chicken's neck and didn't want to. She told me to get on with it and stop complaining and that I wouldn't have survived one day in that British hell, so pampered was I. She had a hard face then, as though it was set in rock, hands that looked as though they would reach to hit me. Instead she grabbed the chicken, its beady frightened eyes shining, and after one swift movement it hung limp in her hands.

"Spoiled us they did, I forget how many times, every day and night you could hear us screaming, then we learned how to keep quiet, bite our lips till they ran with blood. Half starved to death we were, how they could even bring themselves to lie upon us!"

I remember her large capable hands, slitting the still warm chicken's throat, bleeding it right into the sand where we stood in the yard. Her fingers tearing out the feathers, a soft popping sound. I watched her, my stomach churning, the blood and the feathers all sticking together, the claws.

"I got sick, Sarah, right there at her feet and she looked at me without trace of emotion in her eyes and said, "Yes, such things will make you sick."

My grandmother would play absentmindedly with my hair, tell me that her mother was the strongest woman that ever lived. "We can't go wrong, love, with some of her blood in us. Pity your mother married your father."

The sun has gone down already and she has put on a reading lamp and the room was filled with a soft yellow light. I am glad for that, having never liked the twilight much.

See, it's just a case of getting screwed, the men get screwed and, in turn, to express their anger at such injustices, they screw the women because it is easier, takes hardly any thought at all to rape someone, trust me, not a thought was in those who raped me. Brute force is all it takes, what could be easier when you have the physical advantage? Should it ever get to a courtroom you can spin any old lie about provocative dress, or one too many drinks and the other men will slap your shoulders and stand by you, and sadder still, some women too. The women are always luring the men, aren't they? Harlots we are, can't trust us even when we are bound and gagged. Her word against his.

Appalling ignorance is all it is, Imogen, go on say it, nothing more terrifying than a mass of uneducated people believing their ignorance is a way of life, where it becomes their life.

Women have their own history; what do you think our grand grand matriarch was saying in that yard with the feathers and the blood and the stench of chicken giblets? Our history a convenient backdrop to the real history? They took our women! And always lumping us with the children as if we cannot be separate, autonomous beings. Rape and sexual violence are expected causalities of war and conflict? There are no rules in war, nor in peace time either! Our history is swept under the carpet, and reams are written telling us how the men fell and lost their limbs.

Something can and will always be found to justify it. Poverty, emasculation, plain and simple boredom. Anything. Emasculation, what are you talking about Imogen! Women haven't been allowed to be themselves for centuries and we don't go on the rampage, do we? Are we that used to being labelled, so used to fulfilling a conscripted and rehearsed role that we wouldn't know ourselves if they came up and slapped us! Listen to me, Imogen, I am only just waking up to this rage! Evolutionary biologists will tell us it is in our natures to fuck in spite of common sense and decency, and that is all there is to it, according to the men in courtrooms bloated with pride for all the world to hear. As the bones of our ancestors are dusted off and articulated into intact skeletons, they fill in the missing gaps by assuming we have always been divided and one above the other, because Cro-Magnon must have clubbed his mate over the head when he wanted to get laid. At least one thing is true, you never really witness evolution in your lifetime!

Imogen rolls her neck again and I can see she isn't feeling any of this, the words are stuck and she couldn't care anyway, it is a losing battle isn't it then? She swallows another shot of vodka, puts her head on the keyboard.

Nxufcal4r8p9xiuen cuhfncjhf winerziuer874ztnuch fnsljhdklajskalkdjöarj2"1!12111!!!!

Says it all quite nicely don't you think?

I wouldn't mind a drink myself, I hate the nights, nothing lonelier when you only have yourself to walk around with. The days are better, louder and a little safer, but only by inches, mere inches.

My daughter gets up and walks lazily to the bathroom. I can hear her running a bath, I can smell the lavender and tea tree oils, I can hear my daughter crying and I know I cannot follow.

She emerges over an hour later, puffy eyed, a fine steam coming off her bare shoulders. I want to wrap her up in my arms, for the first time I am experiencing a fierce maternal instinct, something so desperate and powerful I am afraid of it, for I can do nothing about it. I want to hold her till she falls asleep in my arms and hold her still, hold her forever. God, why, why am I dead? Some of the pages on her desk are thrown to the floor and it wasn't Imogen, who is looking frightened and pale, at the scattered pages. It certainly wasn't me, or was it?

She inspects the contents of the vodka bottle and decides she drank too much and is seeing things, or it's just a draft from somewhere, though all the windows are shut tight, then just for the curiosity of it she ventures, "Mom?"

I answer her in the affirmative for that is the only thing I could think of saying, but I have no voice, I am as far from her as I am from finally disappearing.

Yes, it's me, Imogen. I am standing right in front of you! Can't you see me? Try, look harder and closer, I am right here! I wish there was someway I could tell her that I was with her, and I have no idea how I made those papers move.

She is drying her hair with a cherry red towel, laughing to herself, that she had even entertained the idea that I could be near her. Laughing and crying, laughing and crying, never matters much in what order. She gets into bed with her damp hair, she will be catching a cold soon. I can hear my grandmother telling me, "Don't be going to bed with a wet head." She was always armed with a jar of camphor or vapor rub, just in case I even thought of getting a cold.

I sit next to my tired daughter who is lying awake, staring at the ceiling in the dark. I try to stroke her hair, but she runs right through my hands. I can't soothe her to sleep and her tears won't stop, soundless and streaming in our little hermitage, curled up against the night.

I have dreams of women marching through my veins, in colourful dresses, in camouflage trousers, sweat pooling underneath their armpits, women in burkas with dust swirling about their pounding feet, eyes dark and glimpsed though slits. My grandmothers standing atop cliffs, hip flasks at their sides, Sunday hats held loosely in their hands and frills buttoned to the throat, great grandmother in a man's shirt and riding breeches, a pouch of tobacco cupped in her hand, the smell of blood on her fingers. The clouds rolling in loud and wet with impending rain, troubled by lightning. One by one the women turn into stones. Stones that geologists will come across one day, try to guess their age. But this is not the ending I want for them. The clouds let go, they warned us, who could have believed any differently? Thunder so loud it split us down the middle, and I watched as the heaving roiling sky turned with birds, wheeling above the stones they buried and buried again.

8

IMOGEN WAKES UP IN A SOUR MOOD, suffering a hangover. She nurses her head over a cup of strong coffee, the hair on her arms sensing a chill. I know she feels me, she just doesn't know it yet. I wish the living weren't afraid of the dead. I gave birth to her, changed her nappies, put plasters on her knees, dried her tears, and here she is, getting the cold shivers over me. I don't know if I should be sad or insulted. I guess we have horror films to blame for our skewed perceptions of the non-living. Ghostly ghouls haunting graveyards, the creaking stairs and a long dead child laughing in empty halls. The dead are always crazy and out to get you, spoil that bit of prime real estate you loved so much because it had character, call it atmosphere. Well I am neither crazy nor out to get you, Imogen, only trying to make an impression, say something to you.

She pages through her diary and calls in sick. They will understand, won't they?

Her superior suggests some compassionate leave. "Take some time," the nicotine battered voice says to her. "We can hold the fort here, no rush." I am still getting used to being privy to what people are saying on the other side of the line. Can hear a pin drop in rush hour traffic if I cared to, or an insect walking on a leaf. It is almost impossible keeping the remnants of my molecules from drifting into other molecules, getting an inside view of what things really look like.

I can see she is relieved, loses the tight expression around her mouth. She pours herself another cup of coffee, takes the mug with her to bed, turns on the television for company. I never knew my daughter was so lonely. There's nothing more depressing than daytime television. It can put you in an instant coma, and when the sun dips behind the horizon you notice you are still in your dressing gown and you haven't got the supper your husband is banking on ready yet.

Imogen flicks through the channels, sighs with tedium. I leave her to it, kissing her on the top of her head before I leave.

Mrs Watson is ringing our doorbell, peering inquisitively through the keyhole.

"Mr Jenkins, William, it's Maude Watson from next door!"

I would ignore the bell too. Once she gets talking there is no stopping her! William, ever polite, opens the door in his tatty bathrobe, the rope tied in a messy knot around his waist. I used to love that bathrobe, wore it on our quiet Sundays, reading the papers and the smell of William right under my nose, mingling with my skin, sandalwood and spices.

"Can't you get your own, Sarah, or wear your own?"

"I prefer yours, love, it's warmer, cozier." And he would come to hold me, kiss me, his mouth tender and generous.

Mrs Watson has a plate in her hand covered in foil. "Morning, William. You know you shouldn't be leaving that front gate of yours open, especially since, well, you know."

William tempts fate with the open gate. Come on my love, come to me, can we take the sadness from our eyes, who knows how it will feel if you could join me, what we could discover without our bodies blocking our way? It's different here, you might like it. We can still do all the things we wanted to. William moves to the side, inviting Mrs Watson, who hasn't stopped talking since he opened the door, in.

"I brought you a hot meal, thought you might need something, some comfort food. Made a roast last night, four vegetables, I hope you like pumpkin. My husband, God rest his soul, never had time for a pumpkin, never allowed me to cook it and I loved it so."

William's eyes are glazing over but he replies that he loved pumpkin, especially fritters.

"Yes, with cinnamon, nothing like it, I still have my mother's recipe, I could make some for you if you would like?"

The old bat, is she flirting with my husband? Buttering him up with hot meals and promises of cinnamon! Shameless. I want to laugh hysterically, except William looks as though he really wants those fritters, his hand already on the warm plate with the roast meat and four vegetables. I can't blame him, he hasn't eaten anything close to resembling real food since that night. It's his belly then and nothing else.

"Thank you, Maude, I appreciate the gesture, don't go putting yourself out, on my account."

"No trouble at all. I remember Sarah and how good she was to me when Frank died, and I didn't care for much of anything, it's the least I can do."

So she does remember, maybe I have been too hard on her, thinking she was a nosy old buzzard, a bit of good in everyone and all.

William offers her some coffee. "Do you have tea?" She takes a hankie out from under the cuff of her lime green cardigan, dabs at her nose. "Funny weather we are having, can't make up its mind, cold then warm. Gives me the sniffles."

I can see the panic rising in his eyes, he only knows how to make coffee, doesn't even know where the tea is kept, but he wants to get this right. "I think so; just let me find it first. Sarah knew where everything was."

"No mind, women always keep order, Frank never knew his way around a kitchen, he literally went pale if I asked him to hand me a plate, as if the cupboard would bite his arm off if he tried to open it! Come let me help you."

William stepped away from the counter and Mrs Watson inspected the tins, lifted lids.

"Aah, see, next to the sugar, right in front of our eyes. Nothing like a cup of tea."

"He handed her two mugs, watched how she made it, how long she let it stand in the boiled water."

"You take sugar and milk?"

"Yes, two please."

She asks him for the milk, looking at him through her spectacles which made her eyes look twice their size. He feels like a little boy helping his mother make something. He hopes the milk hadn't turned and hands her the carton. She takes a precautionary sniff and pours.

"Thank you, you make good tea."

"Been making it for long enough, would be a little sad if I didn't make a good cup!"

Now that they have made the tea, William doesn't

know what else to say and he sips noisily from his cup.

"Shall we enjoy it in the garden William, on the porch? Sarah kept such a lovely garden, will be a shame not to venture into it."

At the mention of my name and what I liked and what I did, I can feel William wince, feel his stomach clench, and his eyes burn. She doesn't mean to be insensitive, she was too old to worry about sensitivities, and rather called a spade a spade. No use pretending anything when you are nearing 80. She gingerly seats herself down on a wicker chair, William crossing his legs like a woman in another.

"Got terrible problems with aphids, ruining my roses, the bloody blighters, I have put so much effort into that rose garden! This is splendid. Sarah, she had a touch, a green thumb." William took a sip of tea, suggested dish-washing liquid or tobacco.

"Heard of that, never troubled myself with tobacco, not about to go out and buy it now. Frank, he smoked a pipe in the evenings, right in the chair next to me while I tried to knit. Made my eyes burn something fierce and when he died that was the first thing I wanted, just to smell that pipe burning."

William nods his head, furiously trying to keep the tears in his eyes from spilling over.

Maude puts down her tea and reaches for his hand, just holds it, not saying anything. William sits sipping and sipping at his tea till there is nothing left.

"If you need anything dear, you'll give me a tinkle?"

He nods his head, adding that my funeral is tomorrow, 11 am at the Catholic church in Mowbray, would she need a lift?

"These old legs haven't driven in years; yes, I w

require a lift, thank you."

She still takes her dead husband's car out of the garage on Sundays, starts the engine, let's it run in the driveway polishes the chrome fenders with her arthritic hands.

"That is a classic you know, Ma," her son-in-law says, always nagging her to sell it to him. "Can't find those anywhere these days," he says, his hands stroking the bonnet.

"Well, what time shall I be ready then?"

William doesn't know, he will have to shower, find a suit of sorts, work up the courage to actually attend my funeral. He will have to be there earlier to receive the mourners, make them comfortable.

"Ten, I guess."

"I'll expect you then, dear."

She is allowed to call my fully-grown and almost old husband *dear,* she is old enough to be his mother. I am grateful that she came, that she cared enough in her small way. I watch her walk behind William towards the front door, a limp in her lift leg, her barrel torso and bandy legs carrying on regardless.

He walks her to the front gate, sees her off to her home like an old-fashioned gentleman.

He is shown the plight of the roses, their stems crawling with aphids.

"Was I exaggerating, William?"

He makes a mental note to sort out the aphids, thinking that he had to be good for something still. He comes back in and sits on the couch, looking at his hands, looking right through them to the cavernous hole on the inside of his head that has not stopped aching. The telephone rings and William, startled out of his skin again, goes to answer it.

It is the inspector, telling him they have found the motor vehicle (police people always speak from their crime and procedure notes) abandoned near Gugulethu. Nothing else was found, no leads yet, nothing. Does he want to fetch the motor vehicle?

William ponders this for a while and answers in the negative: "Sell the bloody thing, keep it, whatever you want to do with it."

The inspector, having nothing more to add, says he will be in touch should any new developments come about.

"Yes, good, thank you, inspector, I must go," and William ends the conversation with a curt goodbye.

He goes to our bedroom, seeing that he was already near, and inspects his wardrobe, trying suits on.

Come naked rather darling, meet me underneath that towering tree with the fat roots and we can get out of here, make the flowers just in time for spring, ride the solar flares because we cannot be burnt anymore.

He tries on a dark brown one that is too big for him; he leaves the trousers crumpled on the floor. A navy blue one with a splash of colour in the form of an orange tie. He isn't sure about the tie but doesn't mind the suit, at least it fits. A white shirt that could do with a lick of ironing, brown brogues, he opts for a pale blue tie, he feels almost human, standing smartly in front of the mirror, we could be getting ready to go out somewhere. William and me.

He undresses again, puts the jacket and pants over a hanger, starts the search for his shoe polish. He doesn't find any, though I could've told him: in the kitchen cupboard underneath the sink. All the other cleaning products are there too, William. He finds an old T-shirt and buffs his shoes with such vigor and fury, he could start a fire, catch a spark. He places them neatly underneath his suit, wonders if his suit could go to the funeral on his behalf. Speak for him from its capacious collar, make the appropriate comments, smile the right smiles while William could curl himself up on the couch and cry himself into oblivion.

Though it isn't anywhere near dark, or any time to be going to bed he lies prostrate on the bed in his underwear, closes his eyes in the late morning sunshine. I lie next to him. It is still my side, still my bed. I find his right hand; think that I can feel it, like tiny electrical shocks, like magnetism drawing particles nearer and nearer. He opens his eyes, shakes his hand, as if it had gone dead, puts it back down again, lies quietly breathing, telling me that he misses me. I study the lines of his face, handsome still with a touch of the rugged, and a slight indentation in the slope of his nose, something that drove me to distraction when we were younger. I was happy to just kiss his nose, wanting to understand how this part of his body could make my stomach do somersaults. I never found the intercourse the ultimate intimate gesture, he could move his hands a certain way while reading a book, or the paper, smile and a dimple would appear on his cheek. It was those things, those public places on his body that I made my own. Here we are, my beloved, marooned on this island, each our own shipwreck, side by side in this drifting room and the traffic outside, turn over, lie on me. I so miss the weight of you. Come, I know you remember, you know this country, these secret places, come for you may, my love. William, sobbing unabashedly, if he could know, into my arms that he turned into, cradling his head in my hands like I used to when we made love. How did it come to this, or it has always been this, just a new war, another story for every generation, burying our own stones?

9

WILLIAM RANG THE BELL at Mrs Watson's gate at ten o'clock. She was dressed in a two-piece black suit, heavy and scratchy looking. Her muddy orange lipstick bled into the wrinkles around her lips. Her swollen feet shoved into sensible square heeled shoes. A red silk scarf tied in a small knot around her neck.

She straightened William's tie, brushed some lint off the shoulders of his jacket. "Well let us be off, then," and she pointed her walking stick onwards.

The traffic had lost its morning rush hour feel and he was thankful for that, not having the energy to contend with that too.

"Lovely morning for Sarah, isn't it William?"

He hadn't noticed it, but it was a day as good as any for a funeral, a clear blue sky, even a hint of spring. The weather didn't match his mood. He wanted the weather to be wretched, streets swilling with water, uprooted trees, angry heartless clouds bearing down on his head. His hands were fists in the pockets of his coat. He wanted Cape Town to remember this day. They wouldn't remember the blue sky, the smell of impending blossoms, and his body already hot and clammy in his suit in the warmth.

Imogen was at the church already, speaking to the florists and the caterers, who were putting the final touches on their sprays of colour and finger foods.

She looked efficient, capable in a long black skirt and chunky boots, an orange shirt with over-sized cuffs. I am glad William didn't choose that orange that tie, it would have been too precious, father and daughter, mirroring each other.

The mourners started to arrive, all traditionally attired in black skirts and suits. They looked an incongruous lot on such a clear and fine day, the hearse with me in it rounding that treacherous corner, next to the taxi rank. A wreath of lilies resting on the mahogany casket. I didn't want such an ostentatious coffin. What was Imogen thinking, all this expense? Maybe it was stained that colour. Good old pine, good enough for me.

She had neglected to arrange beforehand who would be pallbearers, but most were willing to carry me into the church. William, in the front, his face flushed and sweaty-looking, even Mother tottered behind him on her high heels, that strong people coming out in her. Scott Granger, his arms and shoulders broad on account of all the squash he plays. Imogen on the other side of her father, Emily, dear Emily, her mascara streaking already, how lovely it was to see you again. William's brother Michael looked gaunt and thin behind her. Mrs Watson walked behind because she said she wanted to. Who can argue with an old woman?

So many faces I haven't seen, so many turning up for me, where did Imogen find them all? Even the women from my pottery and painting classes, took up a whole pew near the back. The cashier who worked at the supermarket I used to go to; we always chatted while she rung up my purchases. Some of William's colleagues that I recognized, some I didn't, and it is very peculiar to see faces you don't know at your own funeral. My old university friends – we smoked pot and took LSD, saw gnomes in green jackets and red hats, grinning lasciviously at Rhodes memorial. How old we all look now, how very old.

The flowers were beautiful, a small arrangement tied to every pew, larger ones at the doors; the church looked like a garden, too exquisite to feel sad in.

I was laid down as gently as possible, considering the weight of the coffin, in the front of the church. My pallbearers found their places, my mother tripped over a loose piece of carpet, teetering like a spinning top about to wobble on to its side. William held her arm, bringing her to an upright position.

Father Barnard, old and wizened, bringing the funeral service to a beginning. Those who weren't Catholic didn't know when to sit or stand or kneel. One woman that I didn't know remained on her knees for the entire service, in case she was called to kneel again. She would already be there. Mrs Watson remained seated, her legs wouldn't abide that up and down every five minutes!

William got up to stand in front of everyone, clearing his throat for a speech. I didn't think he would, I didn't see him prepare one, maybe he didn't need to. "Firstly, I want to thank all of you here for attending." His voice is faltering already. "To all those who knew Sarah and loved her, we are all deeply saddened by this tragic and senseless loss. I never thought it could ever come to this, always thinking one has time to get to everything. Thing is, there isn't any time, its gone when you turn around again and you find yourself here." He shifted on his feet again, his suit looked suddenly too big for him.

"I was married to Sarah for twenty-seven years and I will always be married to her; nothing can ever change that." The sound of noses being blown and tears running.

William tasted bile in his mouth but he carried on. "She was a devoted mother and a generous and loving wife, a wonderful friend to so many."

Come on, William, a devoted mother? I made so many mistakes, mistakes that I am only seeing now. Yes, I cooked and cleaned for you, made the house a home, but I could have been more, couldn't I? And then there was that time, that long time when... well, never mind.

"I loved her the moment I laid eyes on her, knew I wanted to marry her, back when I was a geeky engineering student and she was burning her bra in philosophy class, saying the lecturer was a sexist pig." A round of relieved laughter.

I did, oh God, I remember that and that shady old lecturer trying to catch a peek at my breasts.

"Sarah died a wrongful and horrible death and I would like to think there is some kind of justice around that will balance this terrible wrong, though it will never bring her back. I can say that all the lights have gone out in my eyes, that nothing much means anything without her and I will surely miss her, more than my own heart can comprehend."

William was quiet, looking at the sea of faces becoming a blur as he struggled to compose himself. "Imogen, our daughter will lead us with the first verse of 'Amazing Grace'."

I didn't know if Imogen could sing. I wondered if she could.

She got up, looking like a little girl at her first concert, took a deep breath and nodded her head in the direction of the pianist. She had thought of everything.

"Amazing Grace, how sweet the sound
   That saved a wretch like me.
   I once was lost but now am found,
   Was blind but now I see."

Her voice made the hole in my middle ache, it reduced all to tears, even Father Bernard, who dabbed at the corners of his eyes. Everyone's voices joined in and soared, just about lifting the roof off of the church.

"'Twas grace that taught my heart to fear,
   And grace my fears relieved.
   How precious did that grace appear,
   The hour I first believed.

"Through many dangers, toils and snares,
   I have already come.
   'Tis grace hath brought me safe thus far,
   And grace will lead me home."

I could see those birds in that sky that I was dreaming flying overhead, burying their stones. I knew I was crying, I didn't need another dead person to tell me that.

"The world shall soon dissolve like snow,
   The sun refuse to shine.
   But God who called me here below,
   Will be forever mine.

110

"When we've been here ten thousand years
  Bright shining as the sun
  We've no less days to sing God's praise
  Than when we first begun."

My mourners stood where they were, except for Mrs Watson and the woman on her knees. They seemed unable to realize where they were, that they were done singing me home and they could sit down now, or file out and eat those finger snacks.

Their heads were bowed, and the silence was deafening. A moment of silence. For me?

Slowly they began to sit, a sound at a time. A final prayer from Father Barnard and then it was over.

My pallbearers carried me out again, back into the hearse, letting go of me, consigning my body to the crematorium's fire. That is what I wanted, didn't want the worms to bore into me, the heavy earth to lie on top of me.

I watched the hearse drive away with me in it, and I realized for the first time that I am done for, that I am well and truly gone and life will go on without me. Knowing that I could do nothing about it I weaved between my friends and my family, standing stiffly on the lawns biting into neat sandwiches and carrot sticks.

Emily was sitting alone on a cement bench next to an Agapanthus that needs tending. She drank a cup of coffee and rolled one of her cigarettes. I always found that attractive, the way she would pick the lost strands of tobacco from her lips. I sat down next to her and watched her fuss with the business of licking the paper, and it wasn't working this time, tearing in places. She lit it anyway, sucking in deeply.

111

I always loved you, you know. The dead are allowed to say these things and now is as good a time as any. She curses the tobacco falling out of her cigarette, stubs it into the pot with the Agapanthus. I never have liked them, always find them in their masses in backwater gardens, old age homes, trying to make the place pretty, standing against face brick walls that time forgot.

You touched something in me I know nobody else could. She would say, "Well, that is too late now, and hell I am so flattered, Sarah."

Not a day passed without me thinking of you, I got so sad without you, even thought of leaving William, but it was difficult then, Imogen a moody and troublesome adolescent, William, I knew I loved him. But I didn't know what you had done to me, love like that, love that I didn't know even existed. He had to go and make it worse by being so understanding, so appeasing, getting me out of bed every morning, though I had a good mind to stay there and never get up again, I missed you so. I assume he thought it was a phase, a curiosity, something that would pass with time. You have never left me.

She drained the dregs of her coffee, the cup pressed elegantly to her lips. A smudge of plum-coloured lipstick on the white porcelain rim. William was standing next to her, asking her if she was alright, could he get her another coffee?

"No, thank you."

He decided to sit next to her, crossing his legs, trying to think of something to say. "Unseasonably warm, isn't it?"

"Yes, it is. Pleasant though." She wasn't fooling herself, there was nothing pleasant at all about the day.

"I am glad you came, Emily, I know it means a lot to her, to Sarah." What he wanted to say was that YOU meant a lot to Sarah, but he couldn't get his tongue around it.

"I wasn't going to come, considering I thought it would be awkward, but I feel better that I did."

She was remembering my hands as she spoke to William, how very convenient it was and innocent that I could say I was just stepping out to have coffee with my girlfriend, before I could work up the honesty: that I was in love with a woman.

"Don't be a stranger," he said to her.

She nodded her head and William walked off, seeing his brother in the crowd, wondering why they didn't see more of each other.

I wanted to hold her, but could only watch her go, walking further and further away from me, her way of walking burning me like branding irons.

You can understand that I didn't want to see myself being shoved into the oven, even I have limits. I don't think I felt it, that immense heat melting the skin from my bones, muscles charred to ashes. Only bits of bone, probably from my femur, fitting into a small cardboard box. I was shocked at that when William brought me home, opened the box, the packet inside the box like a bank bag, fat with my remains.

A heavy groan escaped his mouth and he closed me up again, put me on the kitchen counter, then on the bookshelf; he was looking for some place special. It didn't seem right to him that I should lie in that box next to the groceries, or between a Zen gardening book and a Delft cookie jar.

Mother and Imogen were out on the porch, thinking that my funeral was a fitting send-off. "Never knew you could sing like that, love, nearly killed me, you did." Mother blows her nose, the skin of her nostrils rough and chapped.

"Well neither did I really, that well that is, was surprised at myself, as if someone else was singing through me."

"Tone-deaf our family is, right down the line, flat as planks, except for your great grandmother, she had a voice on her, sang in musicals when she was a young girl, at the local town halls. Her mother had a fit for her to stop, your great great grandmother, hard and mirthless, telling her singing was for some other place and time. How could anyone sing, holding what they did in their hearts?"

"Holding what, Gran?"

"Your mother never told you about the concentration camps, did she?"

"No, she didn't." Imogen wasn't sure if she wanted to hear any of this, her head didn't feel like it had the space to hold anything more. Why did her grandmother feel the need to tell her anyway?

"Well she survived it and your great grandmother was the result of what took place there. Against her will, all of their wills."

"You mean they were raped?" Imogen calling a spade a spade.

"Yes, you could say that."

William brought them both cups of tea that he put down proudly, and, sensing that they were having an involved conversation, left them alone again. Mother took her silver hip flask from her clutch purse and poured a shot of vodka into her tea.

Imogen pushed her cup closer to her grandmother's shaking hand.

"You be careful with the drink, my girl," she said, but she poured a shot into Imogen's tea anyway. Imogen was hardly moved at the words Mother used, thinking she was dropping a bomb into her lap, waiting for shock and surprise.

"The Germans did it too in those death camps, Gran, it isn't unique."

"Always wondered how the world lived after that, and how was love ever possible?" Imogen didn't wonder, she thought it some curse we are all blessed with, to go on when we should rather stop. She had studied sexual violence swept under the rug till the words were just words. No, she didn't wonder at all.

"The world did live after that, Gran, turned its collectively blind eyes on Rwanda, playing football with the heads they had just hacked off, hardly a single woman was spared from rape, those same women having to put families back together again, yet stigmatised and ridiculed because of the unborn children they carried. And the comfort women for the pleasure of the Japanese army in the Second World War, their stories finally seeing the hesitant light of day, the Russians raping the German women, avenging the barbaric treatment they suffered at the hands of the German army, in turn behaving just as abhorrently.

"There are no other histories, Gran, it is the same everywhere, black people were killed too, had their own camps, suffered like the Boers." Imogen was ready to find the racist in Mother, wondering how such shared hardship and misery suffered at the hands of a common enemy could be betrayed years later.

"Well yes, I know that Imogen, but this is her story, doesn't mean we will understand the butchery any better. Let me tell it."

Mother took a sip of her vodka tea, more vodka than tea, and hoped she could tell it to her granddaughter right. Mother had worshipped her grandmother, adored her, and was entirely fascinated by the pipe she smoked; most of the women she knew didn't do that. It was something else too, an admiration of some unearthly strength that her grandmother kept close to her skin, this, more than anything else about her enchanted my young and impressionable mother.

"Of course, your great great grandmother, Adriana, predictably couldn't show her face when the men who had survived were back and broken from the Boer war, what with her belly swelling and no way to hide it. A child out of wedlock was unheard of and brought shame to the families. Ridiculous isn't it? Absurd. Her betrothed sent her packing, saying he wasn't going to raise a bastard child and, worst of all she wasn't a virgin, anymore. She had been spoiled. Didn't matter to him that she had been taken by force and without her consent, well consent has never meant much anyway. What does it mean, being spoiled, anyway? Not like the men had to be chaste!

"So she left, a few belongings in a suitcase and a growing child in her belly. There were some kind people that took her in, gave her a meal and a bed for a few days, but soon the tongues were wagging and what were these respectable families doing looking after a pregnant woman with no husband in sight? She could have told them her husband was dead in the war, but it never occurred to her to lie about such serious things, when there were husbands that were dead. She left before they could tell her to go, knowing that they had extended their generosity far enough."

Imogen drained her cup, asked her grandmother for another shot.

"I was just about to fill our cups, dear."

"She came to a rundown plot of a land, a ramshackle house slanting in the middle, a little girl playing with stones on the porch steps." Imogen was sure her grandmother is filling in the gaps and making things up as she goes along for poetic effect.

"The road had made her hungry, the horrors of the camp had left her thin and gaunt, malnourished, and now there was a child demanding nourishment from her already spent body.

"She remembered the house falling to its side (or was she falling?) the girl bringing her burly father to the stranger lying flat on the ground. The father called for his wife, who came running in heavy skirts and black boots laced to mid calf, scattering frightened chickens as she ran.

"The sky turned above her head and she wondered if this was it, if this was where she would give in, not then with those men ruining her, withholding food, working her into blind exhaustion, killing her fellow women, their children in front of her eyes. No, not then, but now, when life was all used up and she would never see anything beautiful again. She felt herself being lifted, clumsily, dropped onto the ground, the father in a heavy British accent telling his wife to put some back into it. 'There, get under her legs, get a strong hold.' The little girl, Beatrice, tried to help by dragging the suitcase across the yard and up to the house.

"Adriana didn't really know where she was, thought she was back in the camps, that accent, thought they were coming to rape her again and this time she would die. She moaned, cried from eyes that couldn't anymore and never could again. The wife said in soft tones that she should save her strength. She felt delicate fingers stroke her damp face. Then she was lifted again, the yard spinning and wobbling around her, an old mule stood at a fence, by a towering tree she doesn't know the name of. Up the creaking stairs and into the warmth of the house, the smell of bread and grease, clothes drying near the coal stove. A sack of potatoes on a wooden table. Another room and a soft lumpy bed, she was so tired, she didn't want to close her eyes for fear that they would never open again.

"The wife left her with the husband, who took a warm cloth to her forehead. The wife came back and put a greasy broth to Adriana's lips, the taste of a metal spoon on her teeth. She could not swallow and the wife put a glass of water to her lips instead. Adriana managed a small sip, which ran down her parched throat and back up again."

Mother missed her calling, should have told stories for a living. Imogen was positively entranced, hanging on her every word, William was dozing on the couch, my ashes on his chest, rising and falling, rising and falling, like we were sleeping together, the gentlest of sleeps.

"'We will make you strong again.' Adriana heard these words before she fell into a dark, dreamless sleep that lasts for three days. Yes, the Wilsons were good to your great great grandmother. They stayed out of the politics of the time, making a difference where they could. Of course, she hated the child inside of her, growing bigger everyday, a lonely and dreadful reminder of the camp.

"She would sit on the porch in the husband's breeches and shirt, because the wife's dresses were too small for her and they couldn't afford to buy her anything new. Sit with a bereft expression on her face and Mother Wilson shelling peas into an enamel bowl, Beatrice eating the ones that fell to the floor. They didn't have to say anything to each other as they understood. Still, Mother Wilson told her that in time she could love her child and Adriana grimaced into the afternoon sun, not sure if she had it in her to even love a dog.

The labour was long and agonizing, difficult, especially in those times, no woman can really describe it to you, it is something you have to experience yourself, it is your own journey. If we really remembered how painful it was no woman would ever go through it again.

"Mother Wilson kept busy all night with blood-soiled sheets and the howling Adriana, the husband helping where he could but in the way really, going pale and faint at the sight of blood, though he had slaughtered his farm animals with his own knife. Adriana thought she would die from the pain, that no one should have to feel that much excruciating agony, her insides splitting, coming asunder, Mother Wilson's head between her legs, and then it was over.

"Your great grandmother, tiny and yelling, taking her first breaths and Adriana felt nothing, turned her back to the wall, only too relieved that she was finally out of her, while Mother Wilson tried to coax her into holding her, tried to get her to breastfeed her hungry daughter.

"So it went on for two days. Even Father Wilson spoke harshly to her: 'Your daughter needs feeding, it is not right, not natural what you are doing!'

"Adriana replied, 'You tell me what is natural,' her voice dead in the room with the curtains drawn. 'Take the milk out of me then, I just don't want her near me!'

"So Mother Wilson helped Adriana express her breast milk into a glass bottle with a rubber teat, Adriana's breasts heavy and sore. She left Adriana's daughter next to her in the bed, the bottle within easy reach of her hand on the bedside table. She was niggling next to her mother's back, prodding Adriana with her tiny legs. Adriana turned around, slowly meeting the curious gaze of her daughter, her eyes new and indigo blue.

"Adriana had never felt so sad in all her life. How beautiful her daughter was and how she had hated her, how her daughter touched all that was raw and sore inside of her and what did she know, with those old young eyes, she didn't need to know the truth. She could try a little, inch by inch to get closer to her, to warm to her.

"She reached for the bottle, placed it awkwardly into her daughter's mouth until she realized what it was, and started sucking. She was both disarmingly vulnerable and unnervingly strong.

"The Wilsons were relieved that Adriana had finally taken to her daughter, and as soon as Adriana was able, she worked on the land, earning her keep. She ploughed the fields with Father Wilson, learning how to kill and slaughter animals, beating the sheets with a paddle when Mother Wilson was laid down with one of her dizzy spells. Adriana never got back into dresses, preferring the ease of movement the breeches afforded her. She wore a veld hat in the midday sun, her arms lithe and sinewy on account of all the backbreaking work, wrestling with reluctant cows who knew their fate and the heavy plough grinding through the dark soil.

"Your great grandmother, Hannah, learned all she could at her mother's side about farm life, but never did have the stomach for it, and she preferred to play with Beatrice, the little girl growing tall and too big for her dresses. All day in the river they would play, laughing and giggling, and Father Wilson would bring them something sweet from the fields.

"Hannah liked singing, a daydreaming child, losing herself in the fields nearby, singing to no one in particular. It annoyed Adriana, a certain light had never returned to her eyes. 'Get nowhere if you sing silly songs all day child, there is work to be done, lazy you are, leaving your mother to do everything, the Wilson's so good to us two outcasts, and there you are singing as if you had no care in the world.' Hanna would reply, 'But I like singing, Mama.'

"'What's there to like in this world, think the cows and bulls like it when I come to fetch them, think the chickens don't know where they going, always trying to run away, even the pigs eating and eating because they know that is all they are good for. No place to enjoy anything when there is so much death everywhere. You stop that singing now, it twists my guts.'

"Hanna replied, 'No I won't, Mama, you can't make me stop singing.' Adriana's arms flexed; a rope of muscle vanished into her veined hands. 'You can't make me, Mama, I will sing when I want to.'

"You got to hand it to your great grandmother Imogen, she had a will of her own. 'You bastard child, you listen to me!' Hannah could see it coming, but she stood firm, she was confused about what *bastard* meant but her mother was spewing hell from her mouth and she thought now wasn't a good time to ask. 'Little devil, there is nothing to be happy about, the pain you caused me, the pain you know nothing about, everything is dead, Hannah. You will never sing while I am still breathing.' Adriana hit Hannah so hard she was sent reeling to the ground. Her head hurt, her cheek stung as if it had been burnt with an iron.

"'Mama, what are you doing?'

"'Bastard child, don't talk to me now!' But Adriana could already feel her eyes burning with tears that she had never let go, and she wiped them away with her sleeve, turned away from her daughter. Hannah got up, stood nervously at her mother's side, searched for her hand and held it, Adriana's hand big and calloused, Hannah's small and the colour of milk, trying to find some tenderness in her mother.

"'It's okay, Mama, whatever is wrong, it's okay.' Adriana squeezed her daughter's hand, said nothing. 'What is a bastard, Mama?'

"'Not now Hannah.'

"'I want to know.'

"'A child born out of wedlock. When the parents aren't married. An illegitimate child.'

"'Oh, is that all, you made it sound like it was a really bad thing to be.' Still Hannah wasn't really satisfied. 'Is that why I have no father?'

"'Hannah, enough questions!'

"'Please, Mama, why don't I have a father like Mr Wilson?'

"'Your father is dead, Hannah, and you don't go asking these questions again.' Thing is, Adriana didn't know which one of them was Hannah's father, could have been any one of them, and they were all dead inside of her. Hannah made patterns in the sand with her bare feet.

"'What did he die of, was he a nice man, would I have liked him?'

"'No Hannah, NO, stop it now, enough!'

"'But...'

"'Look, he was less than the sand you are playing with, like the pig who just eats and eats.'

"'But Ma I like the pigs, especially the little ones and they always eat if you give them something, like they are friendly. What did the pigs ever do?' Adriana couldn't go any further, but she suspected she had gone far enough because Hannah has a dark circle of knowing spreading in her eyes, a sadness come too soon.

"'I am sorry Hannah, your mama is sorry.'

"'All the more reason to sing then, Mama.' She left Adriana standing there, dumbfounded in the field, and watching Hannah running off to the river, to all her secret little girl places.

"Did Grandma Hannah ever really know, what it meant?" Imogen twirled a strand of her hair around her finger.

"Well, yes of course she knew, how else would I know then, as she grew older, got the sense of an adult in her. What Adriana was really saying, when she

123

could form the words around it, was that Hannah was the product of rape. Made her hard too, though not as hard as Adriana, anyway by the time I was around, a little girl, Adriana would put me on her knee, still never caring for dresses. She would hum to me in a tuneless tone, till I fell asleep, cradled against the soft skin of her neck, smelling of the fields still and pipe tobacco."

"Why have you told me this, Gran?"

Mother suddenly looked old and I was always afraid of losing her, never knowing she would lose me first.

"Why tell anything, Imogen? The stories will stay inside of you then, till you forget them. Just a story, someone's life. Our lives all knotted up and unable to tell one from the other. That's all, no real reason really, we all end up dead anyway, and you wonder what all the fuss was about. All that hardship and struggling, when it could have been different right from the start, if we had had any sense in our heads that is. Here I am, 75, and my daughter is gone. That is a story you keep inside, as no one will read it like you do on the inside of your head, just how much everything means."

Imogen had been grateful for the conversation, however grim its content, it distracted her from the present, from her life now on without me. Would the hole always be there?

"Do you have any photographs of Adriana, Gran?"

"I have one, a little yellowed at the edges, but it is Adriana alright, you may have it, next time when you visit me. You should visit your old Gran more!"

Imogen thought she would, not out of a sense of duty, but because she really wanted to. "I'd best be going," she said, though she wasn't sure where it was exactly that she was getting to. The vodka had made her a little shaky on her feet and all that talk about her dead grandmother and mother had made her feel surreal, as if the present light was too bright, and far too sore to look at.

"You sure, Gran?"

"Yes, don't worry about me love, I'll be fine."

Mother put her clutch purse under arm, made her way to the door with Imogen behind her, stopped to touch the sleeping William's hand, shook her head like mothers do.

Imogen waved at Mother, nosing her way into the road a little recklessly, revving the engine till it whined.

So much for amazing grace, then, she thought as she closed the door behind her and went to her father. Put my ashes some place safer, inside the Delft cookie jar, wedged herself in next to him, his hand stroking her hair half asleep and the day disappearing outside.

10

I WILL PASS THE TIME writing stories then, seeing that I haven't been called to any heavenly service yet and I am still stuck here, watching what is left hang on to threads.

Is it night or day? What is the weather? I can make up anything. Purple clouds in a tangerine-coloured sky, birds nesting in trees, too shy to speak. Mountains growing downwards instead of upwards, the wild sprawling scenery receding away from my eyes, back into the boiling oceans from whence it came. Someone up above sneezes and it is all gone, I know this, have known this all before, said and done.

If the rocks could speak what would they say about all they had witnessed here? Little baby girl born in a rotting stinking sewer, so history always tells us, used up and old before she even learns how to walk. Born to a disadvantage, because they will always find her, no matter her cunning and her sure strides outwitting the enemy, sometime if not in her life then in another's. They always find her.

What a strange planet, she thinks. How very absurd it all is, how very unfair and look at the mess we have made of everything. Did we mean it; did we really mean any of the horror?

She passes an ox wagon stuck in the mud, wheels grinding endlessly with stubborn undeserved pride.

But what about the camps, what about the way we were humiliated, and we fought for our land?

Wasn't anyone's land to fight for, just land on a planet spinning in space. Was it worth all the blood, all the injustice?

The clinking of slaves shackled in irons, down the hills in the fields, the bells ringing, whips cracking. Sing over me, sing over these piercing contours until we all learn how to weep, until we are all sorry for what we have done. Until someone isn't an other, just another, shaking your hand, buying you a drink, moving in next to you, life hard and relentless, sing to me to find the common footing, loud enough to keep my heart open and kind, here in this country coursing through my blood that we loved enough to tell its stories.

The rock garden high up on the cliffs, leaning on their sides, holding the other, and in turn holding the other and so it stretches and encircles her.

Tell me *why* is all she asks, the rocks silent, their clavicle bones braced against the approaching wind.

No use asking them, they're dead.

There is no why, only what we have in our hands and what we do with them.

Is this all, she thinks, all it can come to, back to finding love we never had from the beginning?

What if there is no love here, we, all too tired and dispossessed and afraid and sick of poverty to love anything... too late...?

I don't know about these stories, I don't know what to say, I would rather be speechless, for in the instance that you say something you own the feeling, it takes shape inside of you, the subject, when moments of silence let the words go. Someone is being murdered while you read this sentence, someone is being raped, someone is on the ledge of the night because the day never gave them anything, while the noise carries on outside and people go to parties and watch films, while people live. Be still for them if that is all we can do.

The air is cool and the garden catches the mercury of the moon. It shimmers around leaves, sweeping dark shadows, swathes of silver, balancing precariously on the rim of the universe. I have never felt so alone. I can't go forward, I can't go back. I can't even hold my husband's hand hard enough so that he can feel it. I am tired of being invisible yet I don't expect to become clear anytime soon.

11

MY HEART IS A CHURCH SQUARE on Sunday. After everyone has gone home to pretend to pray and the pigeons sleep in the eaves, beaks in ruffled chests. I am getting used to the loneliness, the brass bells are silent in my lungs. I cannot laugh anymore. All week my family has been making trouble in my veins, my blood doesn't trust itself. All week they have been drinking hard, putting their cigarettes out in my eyes, so that I will never see kindness outside again. Taking me with them, on their wild rides through the city, lit up like live electrical wires, and I look at the passing windows and wonder who is lonely behind them, wonder who sips at a thousand cups of tea, leaving the cups in the sink, because it is only me here. Wondering about that love I never got to.

Breaking some bones in my body because they hit me a little too hard one time, or was it more, I wish I could remember; do I really want to? A woman screaming at me, a line of blood seeping from a wound on her lips, a man smug and pleased, like a shadow over us, the woman and me cowering, and is anyone passing our window on the street, thinking how lonely we are?

So I give my happiness away, make it all cold and just right for winter to wear, hard scratching branches against the whiteout in my head. I wouldn't smell spring even if they put a gun to my temple, even if, yes, even if they came to my bedroom and put their hands under the covers, splaying my legs open for all that ice to see, the pretty snow falling and me a single red stain flying North.

I only sing in minor keys now. Alone. The choirs of my innocence have already lifted the roof and their voices never returned to me, get inside, get inside of me and tell me love still exists.

No one in this dead place passes here anymore, I am an almost old woman on a bench and if I had some crumbs I would be feeding the pigeons just woken up. The hours I always imagined and feared, coming full circle, time on my hands and never forgotten.

I can't say what is real or what isn't anymore, I am living all my known lives, but never the ones I didn't get to – you know, the ones with the happily ever after. Now it's too late, Mother, too late. I never got to tell you how lonely I have always felt.

12

ALFRED CATCHES THE EARLY TRAIN to work. He is dressed in a suit, a waistcoat underneath his jacket. He wears a hat that sports a colourful feather lifeless on its velvety brim.

He is approaching his 28th birthday. He is in the prime of his life. He has his pass in his pocket; this dreaded thing defining him, rubbing him out. He walks to the third class carriage, passing the "whites only" signs, which glare at him in heavy black ink, further erasing him. The whites in their suits and briefcases sit on padded seats, they sit on better things. Alfred's seat is made of hard yellow plastic which is cracked. If he isn't careful the seat catches and pinches his skin. Yes, he knows his skin is sore, it having been insulted for so long. His brothers and sisters the world over are always looked down upon, and scrutinized. He wonders if the looks he gets even see him as human.

"Leave us alone then, if you hate us that much, just let us be. Don't come looking for us at night dragging us from our beds, beating us, setting your dogs upon us, don't go hanging us from the nearest trees and shooting at us with your assault rifles. Let us be." Alfred can't fathom why he isn't allowed to vote. He would vote those brutal Nats out and send them screaming into the sea, be done with them once and for all, and he could walk without being made to feel ashamed of his skin, which is his body, which is him, which he cannot hide.

Alfred passes the places he cannot go: the restaurants, the cinemas, the smart shops, the benches he may not sit on, the toilets he may not relieve himself in. The public transport is divided into classes and, maybe one day, he could feign amnesia and waltz into first class, knowing that the police would carry him away.

"Sorry I forgot, *baas,* forgot about my skin."

"*Dom kaffir,*" he hears all day, spoken at him as he throws bricks that will become buildings he will never enter, only maybe as the cleaner, scrubbing the toilet bowls, washing the laundry, or serving the drinks and having to be friendly. Never being the important guest.

He saves his measly wages, putting them away for better days that never come. His son learns how to eat stones fed to him from the tin spoon of Bantu Education, which lets him know only so much.

Alfred throws his pick-axe deeper into the earth, holding it aloft in his arms, which drip with sweat. He brings it down again and again, monotonous and exhausting. The white *baas* says that he isn't digging fast enough, his mouth greasy from the vetkoek he eats, his beer belly hanging over his belt, drinking from a flask of coffee his wife must have made for him. Alfred could kill him if he wanted to, swing around with that pick-axe, his arms are strong enough to split his treacherous brain right down the middle.

Instead Alfred asks if he may go to relieve himself.

"It is almost lunch break," he is told. He can hold on till then. The *baas* walks away, his belly swings from side to side.

Alfred eats the sandwiches that his wife made this morning. She has gone on the same third class carriage to clean a house in the suburbs. These suburbs with their pretty gardens kept neat by men like Alfred. Dorothy picks up the soiled clothing and scrubs the mess around the stove from last night's cooking. In the bathroom on her hands and knees, the madam speaks to her as if she had the comprehension of a two-year-old.

"Now Dorothy, you know how to use the washing machine, don't you? You know I don't like my jerseys coming out all stretched, and don't use so much washing powder, you know we struggle, money doesn't grow on trees, Dorothy."

"No *Mies*, it doesn't."

Dorothy carries the white baby who is wrapped in a blanket on her back. She sings as she vacuums the carpets. They won't let us eat from the same plates or sit in the same carriages as they do, but they trust us with their children?

Alfred thinking, having driven the people wild and half mad with despair, they will just make another rule to follow, invent another law to keep the people in their place. Would it ever end? A sense of hope collapses before it is even allowed to be truly felt. The freedom fighters' voices would be silenced, and they would be shipped off to Robben Island to dig into rocks with the same pick-axes for all eternity, singing freedom songs, or hanging dead from ropes.

Alfred and Dorothy are almost old. The stiffness in their bones and stones in their bellies can hardly believe the turning of the tide. Nelson Mandela set free, saying

133

never again will anyone be discriminated against?

The endless lines all over the jagged contours of South Africa weep and laugh and dance as people cast their first votes. They have walked for miles, risking hunger and thirst to make their mark.

The right-wingers, fearing war, stockpile ammunition, hoard tinned goods, build bomb shelters, fall off their horses.

The unspeakable joy that made the hair on our arms stand on end and the tears well in our throats sparked a love in our stomachs which turned with an exquisite tenderness. The rest of the world roared and cheered and we were loved again, we were part of it all again. Have we forgotten what we achieved, what impossibly high mountains we conquered?

Alfred doesn't know, lying sprawled on the sidewalk in the dark, his hand clutching his throat, to stop the bleeding, but he knows it is too late.

I'm writing hard and furious from the edge of memory, forgetting how to tell my brain to move, my arms to pick up the pen or dance my fingers across a keyboard. The words dissolve as I think them, just like real ghosts do, into thin air, writing messages in water vapor on mirrors.

13

MEN: ALWAYS TYING KNOTS in stories, thinking they are going sailing.

Imogen drives to her grandmother's house, through the tree-lined streets of Constantia, up a leafy drive way, and parks behind Mother's old bronze Mercedes. She sees a new dent in the fender.

I haven't said much to Imogen on the way, preferring to watch the streets of my childhood go by. My sadness and sense of detachment grow ever larger with each intersection we cross, with every man selling wire, bent and twisted into flowers. The feeling I always had when rounding that corner, when I knew I was only going home and nowhere else to go waves hello to me, greets me on the stairs with a face that refuses to smile.

Mother looks as though she is holding up all right. She draws Imogen into her arms, holds her close for what seems like a long time. I am starting to forget what it feels like to be held. Mother has laid out the tea in the back garden, the trees green and enigmatic, how many times did I forget myself in there? She has brought out the china, the silver cake forks, something bought from Woolworth's, cinnamon pancakes, thick wedges of chocolate mousse cake. The silver hip flask takes pride of place in the middle of the table.

"I thought we needed some sweetening up, love."

Imogen hasn't eaten breakfast; she hasn't been hungry for days and she cannot imagine eating cake at ten in the morning. She swallows the nausea rising from her stomach. "Lovely, Gran. Just lovely here under the trees."

Mother has searched most of the night for that photograph, finally finding it in a box along with her old stockings which she kept in case the Mercedes' fan belt snapped. What was Adriana doing in there, all crumpled and cracked-looking? She had so many photographs lying in unlikely corners and boxes, why would her beloved grandmother be treated any differently?

She has found an old frame, the wood worn and tired; but she thought that it worked when added to the photograph, Adriana having had the same disposition. Wrapped her up in paper she saved from birthdays and Christmases, gold bells and sprigs of mistletoe, it would do.

"Have a gift for you, dear." Mother takes out the neatly wrapped parcel from her roomy cardigan pocket and hands it to Imogen.

She begins to open it, a papered fold at a time.

"Go on, it's not made of porcelain!"

"Well all right, Gran, I am getting there!"

Adriana looks out from the frame, past the eyes of her great great granddaughter, to something else in the distance, her brow furrowed, her hand holding long hair away from her face.

"You have her colour hair, not that you can see it in the photo. Fancy that, all the rest of us blessed with this dull straw, but you and her blessed with flowing manes the colour of mahogany. Obscene, it is, and wholly unfair!"

"I can't help that the genes skipped you, Gran!"

"Skipped your mother too."

Me, the mother, is gazing out of the widow, wondering if birds ever feel cold. The ones in the garden are ruffling their feathers, puffing their chests out; big enough to pat. The wind picks up, always blowing here.

"No, guess you can't help it, but I would've killed for a head of hair like yours, like hers."

The Adriana in the picture might be nearing thirty, Imogen isn't sure. She isn't smiling, but rather looks from the inside to the outside wearing a quietly bemused expression on her face. Possibly a hint of something raw, even sexual. Her slender frame, the heavy linen trousers, the buttons for absent braces, the boots good enough for the fields. The hint of her clavicle bone. Surely men and maybe even some women would have fallen over their feet to just talk to her!

"Beautiful, isn't she?" Mother looks at our long-dead matriarch, wiping a fingerprint off the glass with a tissue.

"I can see some of Mother in her, in her cheekbones, in the shape of her nose."

"You're right, clear as day. I am going to miss your mother so much, never stop missing people, your great great grandmother gone so long and I still miss her, sometimes I can't wait to die just so that I can see them again.

Don't bank on it, Mother, no one has come for me yet! The birds, little robins I think, now buffeted by the wind, their wings making no headway. I don't think I want to be here, but can't think of any other place to go to really. I don't want to see William, sad and descending further and further into his grief, don't want to see the mountain anymore, or ride in taxis. I don't want to see all the things I cannot do anymore. Yes, it is better to be here today, crawling into my mother's jersey that she has left on her bed, the smell of her imprinted on its threads, one pearl, one plain, and maybe with a feat of the imagination I can remember being held.

Mother had written a little card too, in an elaborate shaky hand. "I'm no good with words, Imogen, had to borrow someone else's, my favourite, nothing more to say about the world, reading it in its entirety. It remains all that ever needed, and will ever need, to be said.

Dearest Imogen

I am moved by fancies that are curled
Around these images, and cling:
The notion of some infinitely gentle
infinitely suffering thing.

Wipe your hand across your mouth, and laugh;
The worlds revolve like ancient women
Gathering fuel in vacant lots.
                                        TS Eliot

PS Don't stop singing.
Love always,
Your grandmother

Imogen closes the card, wanting to find words but finding none. The words and the walls and the flowers in the vase on the chest of drawers blur.

"It's all right, love. Come, let's go have some of our special tea outside, if we can with this nasty wind kicking up the place!"

The wind make it impossible to be outside, the napkins keep blowing away; the teacups teeter on the edge of the table. Imogen's long hair annoys her.

I could have told them that. They could lie here with me, the three of us on grandma's bed, talk about anything, laugh about anything, all get silly and drunk if we wanted to. Grandmother had enough vodka to keep even a Russian happy. We could have had a grand old time, just us. We can still remember how to laugh can't we, still remember how to dance to some happy music we used to listen to. Could even light a joint, I'm sure Mother wouldn't mind, has probably tried it anyway. Mother stoned, what would that be like? God, it's all so serious, can't we lighten up, just a little, I so miss it, if I have ever known what light is like.

Leave the sadness where it is, it will always be there should you come looking for it. Can't we do that, just for today? I cannot bear this loneliness anymore, wrapped up in my Mother's talcum-scented jersey. I want to die, but I have already done that! How much dying do I have to do before all of me disappears, before I feel and think my last thought?

They made their special tea. There you go that's the spirit, make it a stiff one, don't go stinting yourself, some things have to be accommodated. It was warmer inside and they sat around the dining room table, a dark and heavy piece of furniture that I would do my homework at when I was a child, kicking my feet against its legs. Mother always telling me to stop it, that

I was ruining her mother's table. I was always ruining something, especially when my father got home and Mother hadn't made the supper right, put too much spice in it, or she just happened to make something he didn't feel like eating that night. Pots and pans crashing to the floor, my mother wrestling with him in the kitchen, trying to cover her eyes, her face, from his striking fists. When he was done and she had to go cooking all over again, something he would eat, I would tip toe into the kitchen, stand at my mother's side, her hands viciously stirring a sauce, asking if I could help her with anything. She would look straight at me, a fresh bruise swelling on her face, her hand still stirring. "No, Sarah, you will just go ruining it!"

"I hope I'm not being a bad influence on you, Imogen, you're getting into the wrong crowd, hanging out with your grandmother!"

Imogen laughed. That sound, so beautiful, so spontaneous, so scarce in her. I keep it inside of me for other days when there isn't any laughter, and I can take it out, from the seams of my skin, where they stitched me up, hold the sound in my hands and how I should have laughed more with you, my daughter. I am sorry for my coldness; sorry for the love you must have searched for in me and didn't find, that rocking maternal love like my grandmother was with me. God knows I loved you in my way.

"Well, *I* didn't know Mother." Is that what you would say, Imogen?

Our countries pulling away from each other – the different worlds spinning in our heads like you said, and you find the world that makes sense to you. Love, warm and giving, never made sense to me. I just grew around what the word might mean. There are things that can ruin you in this life, things you spend the rest of a life trying to figure out. I mean, I don't mean to patronize you, you know what it's all about, how life can go so very wrong and you think you are doing the best with what is left inside of you, think that you are doing the right things. I still don't know, you think I am still stuck here to figure it out, or is this what being dead is really like, for as long as the imagination can stretch to the notion of eternity? I wish you could tell me as I find no answers here.

"Tell me more about Adriana, Gran." Imogen was suddenly curious about her family, when, in the past, she was only ever trying to disown it, or escape it or find another one.

Mother, a smile wrestled from her unaccustomed lips, reached for the hip flask, topping up their tea.

Imogen would be drunk by noon, she never has had a good constitution for alcohol. Mother, on the other hand, can drain a bottle without it touching sides, some hole in her that never gets burned away.

"Well, where were we, at the slanting house with the unfortunate farm animals, the smell of the earth in Adriana's hands, the tree she didn't know the name of? Hannah's bitter realization of how she came about into this world. We found out that Adriana has a temper on her, a hand coming down to strike Hannah's face. We know they go on besides the history, the old bull still straining at the plough she pushes. She doesn't heave anymore when the animals need to be slaughtered, her stomach hardened like iron as long as she avoids their eyes.

"Hannah continued to sing, though seldom in front of her mother. Mother Wilson's dizzy spells became more frequent. Adriana beat the sheets and kneaded dough for bread, her hands just come in fresh from wrestling a beast to the ground.

"Father Wilson's eyes were etched with worry. He sucked hard upon the pipe in his mouth. He could not eat the broth she had made rich with chunks of beef, glassy potatoes, thick slices of bread on the side, pats of butter. The knife and fork were polished to a shine and rested on starched white napkins. Adriana ate, remembering the days when she couldn't.

"Father Wilson knew he couldn't afford the passage back to England, not even if his wife went without him. He thought the harsh South African weather was the cause of her blinding headaches. He laid her down and Adriana drew the curtains before putting water to her lips. Adriana knew she wouldn't make it to the next summer, but she kept her hopes up for Father Wilson, who fretted at the window, leaving the fields to Adriana's capable hands. The doctor came from the sickroom, black bag with a brass clasp in hand, fine dark hairs on exposed knuckles, a suit feeling too warm in the heat of the kitchen.

"The tumour had been there for a while, unknown to Mother Wilson, finding a foothold in the deep folds of her brain. She noticed the lethargy first, trying to reach all the work she had to do, it felt as if she was dragging a boulder behind her, growing heavier and heavier, her vision filming over, blinking her eyes to set it right but it stayed that way. She reasoned that it was the hardships of the time worrying her nerves, and that it would pass and she would get back to all that work she missed.

"The headaches felt like her brain was being split in two, pushing and expanding against her skull and finding no way out. The terrible nausea and Adriana holding her hair from her face, rubbing her back to try and soothe what refused to be soothed.

"Soon she was unable to walk the lengths she was used to, her legs disobeying her at every step, the distance she could move becoming shorter and shorter. The fields vanished from her, the hills she had lain her hand over shielding her eyes from the sun, the yard with the chickens pecking in the sand, that old mule still fascinated with the fence, until her world became mere metres. From the kitchen table to the bedroom and then on to the bed. Long humiliating minutes to make it there. Cups falling from her hands, cutlery too small and delicate for her uncooperative and often rigid fingers to hold. Yes, Mother Wilson's body was under siege, her secret rhythm that had got her up before and busy, now discordant and cacophonous, when the sound gets so loud, so sickening to listen to, Imogen. I guess your body wants to turn it off and flee the orchestra that has betrayed it."

Mother, can't you leave the symbolism. Really, an *orchestra*? Why can't you just say she was tired of feeling putridly sick, tired of puking her lungs out and her brain stabbing her eyes, turning her mad with pain and she got tired enough to die. Sufficiently succinct Mother, we don't need no bloody orchestra and the violin's bow poised over strings.

"It was a clear day when she stopped breathing. Adriana knew it before even Mother Wilson did. She went to her at the appropriate time, held her hand,

143

a fine filigree of blue veins like the branches of that nameless tree, diffusing through her fingers. Mouthing a prayer she used to say in some other place, like a lullaby close enough so that Mother Wilson could hear and then heard nothing.

"Adriana stopped the grandfather clock keeping time, its heavy brass pendulum falling silent and still, closed the staring and always frightened eyes of the dead. Father Wilson sitting on the steps of the porch, his back in spasms, Adriana's hand on his shoulder, the scapula bone, a stump from a wing we remember sometimes. Months passed before Father Wilson joined Adriana in the fields again. He spent most of that time lonely in his bed, or walking to her gravestone, with a view of the hills she had loved so much.

"Father Wilson having moved with Adriana side by side in the fields and in the slaughterhouse since he found her collapsed at the gate, longed for something more permanent with her."

"It was Beatrice, Gran, who found her; not him."

"Men make up their own stories and their own versions. No, in his heart he knew he had found her and not his daughter. She had been so frail, so frighteningly thin, and still some hot coal simmered in the loins of Father Wilson, that he had ignored all that time. He loved his wife, don't get me wrong, Imogen. He worshipped her and never made real with his attraction for Adriana, but he was always tender with her, showing her the ways around the farm, and knowing that her adeptness would surpass his, wearing the seasons closer to her skin than he did.

"So they fell in love then. Or was it just because they were both lonely and he had lost his wife, Adriana

144

a convenient replacement?" Imogen rolled her eyes at the predictability.

"Why so cynical, dear? Not all men look for a gap, I like to believe his affections were sincere and real." Imogen wasn't convinced and I could see her mind grinding with new ways to stave off the possibility of love. I taught her well.

Mother continued anyway, enjoying the happy conclusion she was working her way to. "Adriana was busy shovelling out the shit in the barns, turning it out for compost. Nothing wasted, everything used, even shit, formless and reeking. Wiped her face with the corner of her soiled neckerchief, back bending, straightening, bending, hands sure around the handle of the shovel, the edge of which she sharpened with a stone.

"Father Wilson brought in the pickings from the fields and watched her from the corner of his eye, the sternness in her face, the tangle of hair tied into a knot, so that the nape of her neck, soft and suggestive, made Father Wilson's eyes ache with renewed longing, set his skin ablaze with warmth. He wondered if he could work up the courage to move some of that hair, to bend his head to kiss the angle of her shoulder, put his hand on her arm, draw her nearer to him, draw her in.

"Adriana could feel him watching her, him pretending to be busy shaking the soil clumped around the roots of red radishes, tearing the spent and withered leaves from lettuces, a tingling in her belly, a loosening in the small of her back. She never allowed it, for so long satisfied to polish the cutlery he ate with, appalled at her desire, while Mother Wilson wailed in agony in the bedroom. Appalled that she should feel any desire at all for anyone, she had let those things die a long time ago. Hannah did her sums on a board with a stick of sharpened chalk in the village school, miles away down a dusty road. Beatrice out with her betrothed, square-jawed and docile, at the river.

"Adriana and Father Wilson were alone. They could, couldn't they? Just this once to remind Adriana of giving. Willingly. She handed Father Wilson another shovel and said there was work to do. He looked at her, perplexed and yearning at the same time and said, 'No, the work can wait,' and took her hand rather, gently leading her to pleasanter-smelling surroundings: out through the gate, the mule moving away grudgingly on its hooves, the flies rising then settling again on the scabs of its legs.

"Down a battered path, wild cosmos flowers leaned out and brushed the sides of their swishing trousers, their boots ground the gravel deeper into the path, their fingers explored the palms of each other's hands. A small clearing, softer ground, a young tree with needled leaves provided enough shade, the sound of the river in the distance, sweeping around curved embankments. Adriana's lips to his, her tongue touching the enamel of his teeth, the smell of the radish he had eaten in the fields, dusting it off on his trousers, sharp and clean on his breath.

"Adriana touched further, the moist inner sides of his mouth, and found she is still afraid to let go, to give in, she wants to put herself inside of him, but finds she cannot go deep enough and the sky tilting, the hills oblique, then horizontal, her hands in his hair, his cupping her breasts, touching them as if they were hymns he knew the words of. He was gentle, he took his time, she took hers, astounded that she found tenderness in her hands, undoing the knots inside of her, making way for him, letting him. Her eyes found his and pulled such sadness out of her – such heavy things – the sound of her in the places she never meant to remember again. But she always did. Her arms held him tighter, around his bare back. Letting all her voices go."

Mother took a deep breath, her shoulders rose and fell, she took a sip of vodka sans tea.

"Of course, there was no stopping them after that, fucked any time the mood took them, which was often."

Imogen raised her eyebrow at Mother's choice of words.

"Behind closed doors, when Hannah was home from school, working on a comprehension exercise at the kitchen table, her letters skew and blocky. In the stables, the animals curious witnesses to their incendiary passion, there in that soft clearing where the sky had moved on the inside of Adriana's eyes. Heavens, dear. Don't look so shocked. We fucked back then too.

"The farm suffered some in their salubrious absence: the chickens wandered around the yard confused but happy that none of them had had their necks wrung yet, the old bull came wandering to the plough, its muscles grown flabby, easing himself onto his haunches, not knowing what to do if he wasn't going to be pulling a plough today. Animals grew fat and content at Hannah's hands, happy that Adriana and Father Wilson had lain off killing them. Hannah began naming them, names like Bettie and Winifred. The animals, they couldn't trust the strange turn of events, the known rhythm of the farm out of kilter. Some of them walked to the slaughterhouse of their own accord, milling in front of the heavy wooden door that took all of Adriana's strength to pull open, the animals at the entrance, catching the piercing glint of the hooks hanging there, the long butchering knives, meticulously sharpened so that their deaths didn't smart too much. They wandered back to their paddocks, a sense of dread in the whites of their eyes.

"Hannah tired of eating sandwiches that she had to make herself, spread with butter turned rancid, tending best she could to the garden going to seed, eating around the worm-eaten holes in the radishes. Beatrice was too busy at the river to think of anything else. Hannah, hungry for something more substantial, took a chicken in her hands, its wings and feathers fussing and its throat squawking and she wondered if she could do it. She wanted to let it go, so scared was she of it, its pimply legs and yellow claws scratching her hands. She had watched her mother do it many times, not that she wanted to, her mother just adamant that she had to learn these things. It had to be quick, no time to wonder what its legs or its claws were doing, no time to wonder what she was doing, the warm neck soft and vulnerable twisted in her hands. Hannah threw the dead chicken down as soon as it was over, repulsed by it, repulsed at herself. Now that it was dead she had no idea how to go about plucking its feathers, cutting its throat to let the blood run out. Hannah retched and got sick, her hands in its warm moist innards, pulling them out, dropping them to the ground.

"'You will be ruining good eating, Hannah.' Adriana, emerging from the bedroom or the field, the paddocks. She was thinner, her face softened by what had kept her away so long. 'Come, let me help you, child.' Adriana made quick work of what Hannah had started and it was in the hot oven before Hannah could find the will in her to get sick again. This time her mother made her a tea drawn with slices of fresh ginger, 'To settle your stomach,' she said.

"Father Wilson lit his pipe, telling no one in particular that he was positively ravenous with hunger, and asked in a jovial manner if that harlot daughter of his was ever going to come home again. So the farm went back to its accustomed rhythm, the fire in Adriana and Father Wilson having cooled to manageable embers, though sparking with renewed vigour any time they chose. The old bull was happy to be ploughing again, the animals expecting their fate, digging their hooves in, pulling at the rope Adriana was pulling from the other side, Hannah learning not to retch."

"Did Beatrice get married, Gran?"

"Beatrice? No, love, never made it there, caught a consumption of sorts, months spitting blood and growing thinner. Father Wilson cursed death and his rotten luck as he dug her grave, right next to her mother, though she had always cared more for the river than for the hills. Adriana never married Father Wilson either. Them preferring to live around and inside of each other, having become accustomed to it. Father Wilson thought if he married her something dreadful would take her away, a raging fever, coughing fits, another tumour and he couldn't live through all of that again. She never had another child after Hannah, something gone barren in her and he, though he might have wanted another child, never made her feel any less for not bearing him one.

"Of course, they were the outcasts of the village and Hannah had endless trouble trying to find a man to court her, the families suspicious of her background; the beautiful young woman, her paternity a mystery and a mother living out of wedlock with a widower. No, they had imagined better things for their sons. You could see the disappointment in the sons' eyes, but their fathers were stern, patting their paunches in stiff heavy chairs. Their mothers were even sterner, their hair swept into buns and brooches clasped at their throats.

"A man, lithe and handsome in an audience, watched, listened to Hannah sing, loved her the very moment she opened her mouth and made that sound come out, otherworldly and disarming. He was smitten, sending her roses and coming to every performance. Hannah only too happy with all the attention, loving the way he smiled at her.

"It was not long before she found herself at the village altar and the bells in the belfry rang, Stefan, your great grandfather smiled broad and proud, in coattails. Hannah wore the late Mother Wilson's wedding dress, Father Wilson saying she would have wanted it that way, and Hannah was like a daughter to him too. Mutton sleeves, silk-covered buttons, strings of pearls, her hand squeezed Stefan's fingers as they said their vows. Adriana was in a smarter pair of trousers, a black velvet jacket, a spray of lace from the cuffs, almost shedding tears, Father Wilson crying.

"There was the question of what they were going

to do, now that they were married. Stefan, loathing his job as an office clerk, had big dreams for farming. Having lost both of his parents in the Boer War, there was a bit of money they had kept aside for rainy days, but it wasn't enough. Father Wilson talked to the young and optimistic Stefan at the kitchen table about the miseries of farming, 'A hard life son, any romantic notions you got, put them to bed.'

"He couldn't be dissuaded and seeing that the weather had been good to Father Wilson and Adriana for a change, they helped the newly weds buy a farm: a large one going for a good price – the agent was convincing, his white teeth flashing and the pen in his hand.

"They struggled the moment they set foot on that land, the ground so hard and full of rocks it was hardly worth the back they put into it, turning the soil, breaking up the rocks over and over again till some headway was made. Adriana with her old bull, Hannah with a shovel, Father Wilson and Stefan with pick-axes, the sun blistering over their heads. Stefan, not wanting to send any animals to the abattoir opted for dairy farming, started out small. One hundred jersey cows. He and Hannah and the hired workers, knowing more about the land then Stefan did, put all their hands around the udders, squeezing, pulling, expecting the milk yellow and warm but coming out streaked with red. The workers saw it all shot to hell, but Stefan, not letting a bout of mastitis quash his resolve, quarantined the ones that were sick, medicated them, sold the milk that came out right. He was making a loss before he even started. Hannah, the tiny bud in her belly swelling, had worry in her eyes.

"The cows got well again, the milk from the udders creamy and frothy in metal buckets, the ground turned around, becoming dark and loamy. Father Wilson was surprised at the determination in all of them, even the cows hell-bent on getting better. Stefan thought of expanding, of turning a profit and purchasing more cows and a prize bull for a hefty price from the auction. Stefan wondered why none of the cows were falling pregnant, the bull recalcitrant and stubborn, eventually mounting an uninterested cow and then another. Stefan waited, the workers starting to laugh at the bull chewing cud in the field. Adriana couldn't help laughing at the cruel irony, that Stefan had purchased a sterile bull. Had good shoulders though, good for pulling, and her old bull was just about worn out.

"Stefan went to look for that sterile bull, shouted and cursed at it from the wire fence, its gormless face looked back at him, a grunt flared from its nostrils. He threw his veld hat onto the ground, and stamped on it in a fit of rage. Adriana came running, arms wild like a scarecrow to the fence, fetching Stefan. There was blood running down Hannah's legs in the outhouse. Stefan left his trampled hat in the dirt, his shirttails flapped, sprinted up the winding path, Adriana behind him, her heart pounded in her breast."

"Hannah suffered three miscarriages and Stefan wondered if that blasted bull wasn't a grim messenger for sadder things, things he hadn't reckoned on, things he hadn't stitched into his dream, which he imagined filled with children. The women on the farm told Hannah to do handstands, make love only when the moon was full, gave her dark and pungent herbal mixtures to drink, which only nauseated her. Told her the snake inside of her was spitting out the seed.

"Stefan became more downcast as the months passed hopefully then ended again, nearly breaking that old farm bed, putting every effort into conceiving and keeping that child. Hannah carried to term, the pregnancy filled with worry and Stefan treating her like a wounded bird, not allowing her to do anything that would strain her, that would send the blood rushing again. With all the struggles on the farm, at least they had my arrival to celebrate – my mother Hannah sent one last howl out into the night and there I was. Adriana always told me that she was the first person who held me. A sense of hope again for Stefan, for Hannah, thinking that I was a miracle sent from heaven, they named me Angela.

"Adriana gave her old bull to Stefan, taking his sterile one to work the fields with her. The old bull never dreamed of such a retirement, let loose in a field of cows batting their long lashes at him. He had thought that he would be pulling that plough till he heaved his last. Calves on wobbly legs in the spring and me in my mother's arms on a rocking chair."

The morning and most of the afternoon had disappeared into dregs at the bottoms of tea cups by then, Imogen slightly drunk and worn out from all the listening, Mother rubbing her arthritic legs, which had gone to sleep, me having come down from the bedroom, sitting at the table, next to Mother, kicking through the tables legs, hearing things crashing to the floor. Mother quiet and fiddling absentmindedly with the lace patterns on the tablecloth. "Where do you think your mother would like to be, Imogen? I mean her ashes, did she ever say anything to you?"

Yes, people always say those things, things like, "When I go I want to be cast into the ocean, or from that cliff I climbed that spring, or in a field yellow with sunflowers, from my lover's hands. What about just on top of the mantelpiece in a pretty bottle so I can keep my eye on you, or under the kitchen sink? Any place, really, it doesn't matter." Me, I never said things like that, I never thought about it, never thought that there was some special place inside me I would want to be returned to once I got to leave.

"No, she never said anything. Dad has not said anything about it. Yet, that is." My ashes. And they sound so normal as if they were discussing what to buy from the grocer!

"He can't go keeping her in that cookie jar, it doesn't feel right, Imogen."

"Probably wants her to be near. Like we all do, Gran."

"Yes, I know, terrifying how death is so empty of the person that was there a second ago." Mother worried her cardigan sleeve for that bit of tissue she had used to wipe the glass clean. She pressed the tissue to her eyes, as if that could help the way they hurt. A sigh escaped from her lips.

"Your grandmother is tired. I need a lie down, a nap, getting old, dear."

Imogen took this as her cue to leave, wanting to be alone too.

She backed the car out of the driveway, just missing a potted geranium, Mother's hand waved goodbye. I told her to concentrate, I don't like the way she has to squint her eyes to see the road, the wheels crossed the line, corrected again, a blank expression on her face as the white streetlights come on and go out across her cheeks.

They will lock you up and throw away the key if they stop you, ask you to breathe. Do you want that, Imogen, in prison becoming some thick-armed woman's bitch, or worse still, take to reading the Bible, picking up a ball of wool and needles?

I thought she would be going home but she stopped the car in front of William's house, scraping the tyres against the curb. "Fuck," she said, as she got out and peered at the passenger side, found nothing wrong, stepped onto the sidewalk into shit. She hadn't noticed on account of the sky gone dark.

Funny that, calling it William's house; I am disappearing, then, after all.

She rang the bell at the gate; her father pulled open a curtain upstairs. Imogen stood nervous in the street, stood there watching the shadows, waiting for her father to let her in. He asked her what smelled so awful, and she inspected her boots, swore again, took them off, a hole in the left toe of her black sock. She left the boots outside the front door.

William looked concerned about the way she didn't seem steady on her feet and offered her something soft to drink, didn't wait for an answer and put the kettle on for tea. She lay on the couch, untied that hair of hers, closed her eyes, asked William where my ashes should go.

He dropped a teaspoon, bent to pick it up, the blood rushing to his head, hands on the counter steadying himself. "I haven't thought of it, dear, I mean I didn't think I had to just yet, I don't think I want to right now."

"When you want to, where do you think, Dad?"

"Why is it so important, right now this minute? I want her here with me, I want Sarah with me." He stirred noisily at the tea, his hand shaking with rising anger.

Imogen backed down, took the cup from her father, slurped at the tea, asked him if she could sleep on the couch.

"There is your old bedroom, you know. You don't have to sleep on the couch," he says to her.

"I am fine here, thank you."

Imogen was asleep before she finished her tea. William covered her in a blanket, and looked at her like he looked at her when she was born, telling her that he loved her though she didn't hear him. William took a bottle to bed with him, too early to sleep, looking for an old record, weeping turning around the walls at 33 revolutions a minute, his mind streaming through the irises of my eyes.

14

I KNOW WHEN THEY FIND ME, when they come to cut me open, they will find nothing but words.

Imogen wakes up with a pain in her neck, the cushion underneath her head lumpy and uncomfortable, the clothes she slept in creased and stale. She struggles to her feet, with a throbbing in her head, deciding that Mother is a bad influence on her. Making coffee in a daze, she sips gloomily at the red rim of the cup and pours a cup for her father who is still asleep, a dusty yellow line of sun filtering through a crack in the curtains, the needle still in the record. She goes to splash her face, toothpaste promising to turn what has gone yellow white again, squeezed on her finger, slow disinterested circles in her mouth. Spits.

Neatens her hair with one of my brushes, strands of my hair still wound around the bristles.

Lets herself out, aiming the keys at the table in the hall, far enough away from fashioned hooks, handles through open windows, looking for a way in. Finding her boots, she digs the offending odour from the tread with a stick, rinses with the hose, green and always in a knot, puts her nose to the sole, the smell now faint enough to wear.

She is on her way back to some work she had started a month before I died. That compassionate leave, pressing her into corners asking, "Are you going to get around again, get into the swing of things, drawing on that board again?" Like everyone does.

Leafing through papers in her car, on the backseat, files and folders, thick heavy books, take-away coffee cups. She finds the clipboard she is looking for, fat with dog-eared papers written in her hand. She had been excited about the work, told me about it over tea. Hoping that she could make a difference maybe. She had always been wary of words like that, often glib and self-righteous, never really believing a difference could be made – it involved too much pulling and pushing and smashing convention.

But she had said, "One step at a time", a means of understanding, even if she ended up not helping, at least she would end up knowing.

I had worried about it, why couldn't she just shack up with Bob in the house with the window boxes? I was afraid of losing her, whoever went there of their own accord, like some warrior woman, trying to make that difference.

"Don't worry, Mom," she had said. "I can't not do it, can't not go there."

I smiled at her, weakly and unconvinced, giving up the idea that I could change her mind.

Yes, I remember this place, with the laundry strung between buildings, buildings decaying into the ground, misery silent and taught, accommodated, made way for.

A woman meets her at her car, parked in a sandy rust-coloured square, the woman's body is thick at the arms, loose flapping skin underneath short floral sleeves, she smells of lavender and baby oil. A skirt the colour of red wine, fraying at the edges, reaching her swollen knees.

She has the disposition of a battle-axe; you could imagine her throwing the javelin, or getting a good swing around shot put on an athletic field. Greying hair, frizzing out at the ends, a toothless smile, her lips sunken in on themselves. Skin the colour of strong milky coffee. Tannie Piep, everyone calls her.

She hugs my daughter, asks her how she is. Imogen doesn't tell her that she has been pretty crap, thank you, that her mother was murdered last week and her father is drinking himself into an early grave, but she gets up, gets busy because of Adriana, thinking some of that determined blood must be in her.

Instead, she tells her that she is fine, had a bout of the flu, to explain her reddened eyes and the dark rings that Tannie Piep is examining, her thumb rubbing Imogen's cheek. "Lovey, you look sick," she says. "Come, I make you some tea."

They walk down paths littered with the detritus of hands that don't care anymore, hearts gone old and gone to seed. Up a rusted steel stair case, clanking footfalls up and down, the smell of cumin, curry powder, frying with onions in a metal pot. I imagined the air on Sundays, formless and without a throat to even scream. Not here the sound of sprinklers wetting privileged lawns, nor the shade of smug trees, the colours of guffawing flowers in manicured beds.

Passing clutches of men, swaying drunk and boisterous, cupping hands around brown bottle necks, caps pulled to the sides of their heads. Women sitting on crates, staring, drawing out a sentence sometimes in the sand around them, children in clothes too big or too small trying to play at their feet. What do you mean to do here Imogen?

Tannie Piep unlocks her front door, paint peeling grey and red inside of sky blue walls. Her home is just as I imagined, a small television set, a crocheted cloth, pretty roses stitched between threads of white. A porcelain swan on an imaginary lake, pointing west, heading out of the window, rubbed to a transparent shine with a yellow cloth. A couch, brown fabric, the seats shiny with age, curved wooden arms merging with stout legs. Words embroidered in a frame: *Me and my house will serve the Lord.*

A square table resting on a tatty olive-coloured carpet. Spices and tea bags in orange plastic containers lined up on the sill, labels in black ink. Tannie Piep is in the kitchen, boiling the kettle on the gas stove, the sound of steam screaming through a pin hole. Imogen sits on the couch, checking the sole of her boot again, still smelling something, hoping that Tannie Piep doesn't.

"Here, my lovey, nice and hot, put some colour back in your face." Tannie Piep, a tray in her hand, delicate cups on gold rimmed saucers, cookies with red jam centres arranged on a plate, setting it down on the table.

Imogen thanks her as she tries to wipe the tiredness from her eyes, rub it out of her skin, still smelling the sleep on her shirt. They get to talking, Imogen taking notes with a pen.

"The drugs is a big problem here, all day, all night, nothing better to do." Tannie Piep sighing into the folds of her blouse.

Aren't drugs a big problem everywhere? I had always thought that, half the world on cocaine, on booze or cigarettes, on something. Everyone gone cagey and unpredictable, and, who are you now, you weren't like that a moment ago? So very different that no one could talk you down from any bad idea, any gun you got in your hand, any girl you are going to take, any plan festering and stewing in the fucked haze of the day, waiting for the shadows to make it real.

"The gangs, *aagh*, I don't know anymore, I try so hard, lovey, to get them right, get some sense in their heads. It is a lonely job, the other women too, we try all the time, us older ones. The younger ones only happy to be their girlfriends, getting presents, getting pregnant. My daughter, she is a girlfriend like that, seven months pregnant. You know, I got so mad at her, but what can you do? She is my daughter and I help her. I found that no-good boyfriend of hers, went at him with a stick because I am not afraid of him, or afraid of his friends, laughing at him as I am giving him something to think about. When I die I know where I am going." Tannie Piep's eyes glancing at the embroidered words. Imogen nods her head politely.

"You know, he has found some other girl now, dropped my daughter just like that when he found out she was pregnant. My boys probably would have done the same if they got that far, maybe I taught them better. One dead from the gun of a rival gang, another on a slide, got in the way of cross fire. He was only nine years old; it's this lot in my life that makes me try, and did I try! Lorenzo, getting into that bad crowd, young and angry, and he wanted some place to go in this place, somewhere to belong, you know *mos* how boys are. Went too far, and me up all night wondering where he was and then I didn't have to worry anymore. Sad that I think sometimes, maybe it was better, before it got so bad, like it gets with the others I am trying to help. Mervin, well, he still had a chance to make good, maybe, but they both hurt my heart the same. I worry for Esmeralda. She used to have dreams. Not anymore.

"The other ones, still alive, their brains rotting and looking older than me before they are twenty from all the Tik, kids in school on it, doing anything to buy more, feels like there isn't any hope around here anymore," Tannie Piep, stopping to bite into a cookie, wiping the crumbs from her bosom.

Imogen wants to talk to some of the gang members if possible, Tannie Piep knowing every corner of this round place obliges, puts on a fleecy jacket before locking the door, the air around her turning suddenly cold.

Down the stairs again, greeting people as she descends, Imogen returning smiles. Tannie Piep chastising the ones who look like they are up to no good, shifty expressions in their eyes, "*Haai, wat maak jy? Gaan soek werk, gaan bid; jy gooi jou lewe weg!*"

Imogen notices that the men are wary of her, slinking further into their pockets, telling her that they have been looking, they just haven't found anything yet. The girls didn't have it any easier, Tannie Piep telling them she knew what they were up to, wearing their mothers' make-up, hiding behind walls with men wearing gold chains, holding the girls down with tattooed arms, making babies their mothers have to look after.

Tannie Piep leads her to a room with corrugated

iron walls, a man at the door smoking a cigarette, pressing it between thumb and forefinger, fingers heavy with gold rings, red shiny stones. He greets Tannie Piep, stares at Imogen, wondering what a white woman with a clipboard is doing in the Cape Flats in gangster's paradise.

Tannie Piep asks him if they can come inside to talk, saying that Imogen is from the university, doing research. The man is skeptical, but smiles at her anyway, "*Ja*," he says. "Come, come see." He opens the door and smoke and laughter and voices high as kites tumble out.

Imogen is afraid and she is trying not to show it, as Tannie Piep says, "Don't let them see you are afraid, don't let them think they are on top." Imogen doesn't find it that different from the advice you are given just before you walk into a cage or following the spoor of something dangerous: stay downwind or they will smell your fear.

This looks like a social, some impromptu club built with the materials that were lying around, maybe watching football on Saturdays, clinking beer glasses and waving flags. A hermitage. Except the atmosphere having escaped bears down on you from nowhere saying this is going to hurt.

Imogen knows where she is, afraid of seeing anything different than the violence they are, turning it all grey and then anything can be excused and reasoned – pardoned; makes her want to leave the words, coiled and knotted into each other, trying to find the straight line she doesn't want to cross.

She and Tannie Piep find foldout chairs. Tannie Piep visits often, trying to preach the Lord, trying to preach another road. Imogen doesn't know what to ask them, suddenly feeling horribly embarrassed that she should even be here thinking she can understand any of it. They pass the bottle neck around, sucking hard and breathing out plumes of blue smoke like dragons. You would fear nothing in the world if they were on your side.

Imogen asks about the violent reputation of the gangs. They laugh, saying that violence is the only way to move up the ranks. It is a closed system, then, existing only for itself, violence for itself, proving masculinity? Imogen isn't satisfied, and questions why the system is based on that, that that is the only means to move forward within the system, the hold so strong that they would rather admit to crimes not committed and land back in prison, puppets of the prison gangs.

"It is how it works *mos*." They aren't forthcoming with information on how it works, keeping their secrets and codes close to their skins. "If you don't follow an order, there are punishments. They kill you. Easy." I recognize that voice, the accent. Right next to Imogen, reclining in his foldout chair. Free.

I stare straight into his eyes, darting all over the room, itchy and restless. Try to hold it long enough to climb back into my own eyes that look at him wide with terror, pleading not to be killed, trying to come back from the million points of lights and the loneliness I have crossed, back down from that ceiling into my arms and my legs, back to that view of the garden, but all I can do is howl from some place that had no centre anymore.

I want to shake Imogen, want to grab her hand and pull her out of there. What if he drew that gun he was cleaning and put it to her head, holding it like some American gangsta rap star? Not even our gangs can be original. God, Imogen, run, please. Call the police. Tell them you have found one of the men, tell them to hurry, they can smash down this place, break through the doors. But I know they are not coming. They will not take him away in cuffs any time soon.

She doesn't hear my shouting, I may as well go back to feeding the pigeons or whatever I am still supposed to be doing here. I can't look at him anymore for fear that I will finally disappear.

Imogen asks about the guns, so meticulously cleaned and oiled, the men smearing their fingers with wood glue so that their prints don't show.

"The police don't do nothing. We can show them our guns, give them some money and then they go away again. Easy." Anyone can be bought, then.

They tell her about their wives and children, fathers and husbands trying to make a way out. My man, his eyes on the borders of tears, tells her that his wife got killed in some rival shootout, his little boy too. He says religion helps him to carry on, a sudden hard and deep breath, peering his eye down the barrel of his gun.

Am I supposed to feel sorry for him now, have some compassion that he took my life away, like its okay, I understand he did it? You were wrong weren't you, can you admit that much? Can you?

"This is the dumping place." They are all in agreement. "We were always nothing, not white enough, now not black enough, we are always pushed to the bottom, and we try to get something back. Apartheid took us from our home in District Six and dumped us here in this hell and forgot about us."

What would we have done if the tables were turned on us and our white skin? The government of the past ignoring the social and intimate importance of family. The government – it assumed that coloured folk don't love, and that it wouldn't hurt a bit of course to be moved to some other place. It threw them away, over a cliff, and when they crawled back up again, mad and enraged with misery, it said, "Yes, but that is how they are you know, heartless and savage – you see that we weren't wrong."

So I learn to turn in the scars he made in me, learn to turn in the scars I made in him. Meeting his eyes again, though he can't see me. I don't want this yet; my anger makes sense to me, it is a known country and I know the animals there. Imogen, shifting uncomfortably in her metal chair, knowing she can't hide the colour of her skin, wishes that she could.

Tannie Piep coughing from all the smoke billowing from the pipe, her eyes streaming with tears: "That stuff is a *gemors*," she tells them, indicating the bottle neck.

"*Ja*, but we can forget all the misery of our lives *mos*, Tannie Piep."

The conversation seems to have come to some uncomfortable ending, Imogen not knowing what to ask anymore, the men high on drugs, the atmosphere charged and potent, she needs air. The fine hairs on her neck bristling – must be because I am standing behind her.

Tannie Piep folds up her chair, puts it back in its place, tells them to do something useful, stop being little boys playing with guns. Well, Tannie Piep knows they don't play with them, but sometimes she is tired of the words, tries to think they have just lost their way for a while but will come back if she speaks like a mother to her son, his hand in the cookie jar.

Imogen thanks them, they didn't have to talk to her and she found their willingness surprising, finds the way that their violent notoriety could be quieted into a conversation disarming.

She declines another offer of tea, Tannie Piep, looking disappointed, tells her to come again soon, that there was work to do. Hugs her goodbye.

The man I know making his way up a staircase in the distance, untouchable – alive. Imogen, kicking up gravel, makes her way to the main road busy with noise and life still existing against all the odds.

She is suddenly exhausted, the lethargy hitting her hard and she struggles to keep her eyes open, eyes on the road in the midday sun.

It takes all of my energy to hold him steady in the line of my sight.

15

IMOGEN: FRESH OUT OF THE SHOWER wrapped in a dressing gown, fingers at her keyboard. A shot of vodka to get rid of that headache that has been gnawing at her temples all morning.

The violence expressed in the gangs of the Cape Flats is disturbingly homogeneous. This homogeneity contributes to the normalization of violence and fear within the communities, where people of the community learn to live side by side with the gang members, perpetuating tolerance and acceptance.

Isn't everyone tolerating it? In the squatter camps, the suburbs, everywhere, each community afflicted with their own kind of misery their own anger, lashing out wherever possible? Victims of crime wearing their incidences like badges. "Hey, you were lucky to come out alive, or unscathed, unlike my friend who didn't make it. Be thankful." The naturalization of the unnatural?

Where have you been? This is nothing new, we have been killing each other further back than anyone cares to imagine, ancient battle wounds in those unearthed skeletons, cataloging our barbarism, thinking we must be different now, appalled and embarrassed that we aren't. Hoping, that because we learned to cry somewhere in between, baffled at the stars or the sudden rush of compassion and sadness for that someone or something we had killed, what did those old bones feel the first time they put their fingers to their face, discovering it was wet? Something to get over and get used to and easy to wipe away. We are sorry for how this is going to hurt you but you can understand, can't you?

Anyone can talk too, Imogen, that wasn't a conversation, that was an automaton, moving his mouth, the same worn-out record going around in his head – gotta fuck, gotta kill, gotta prove I am a man, gotta make it all turn to shit because its what I got. I might have dropped off to sleep if it wasn't for him, sitting right next to you, sucking on that pipe.

What is so endearing and so touching about being a father or a husband? Anyone can play at that, doesn't mean he lives up to the labels. All their talk made it look like it was something unique, that there must be some good in their guns if all of that mundane normality still piques their interest. So we can all say, "Well, you know, they have families to look after and it's different for a man if he finds nothing to do, if he gets pushed against a wall. I have never gone hungry, I have never lived in a dump, what would I know about what I could be capable of if I ever found myself there? What boundaries would I cross and excuse? But why kill me? I could part with everything I own, just leave me my life."

Imogen begins doodling with a pen on a piece of paper, her focus waning. She doesn't seem to be concentrating lately, distracted and restless, preferring to lose the hours in her shot glass.

She listens to messages on her answering machine, her father thanking her for the cup of coffee, and she could come around later if she wanted to, he was at loose ends, or didn't know what to do with the ends. William, making light with his pain. Mother asking her out to shop for a spring garden this week: "Lovely new roses, dear, some herbs for the kitchen, will do us good to make something pretty." A man with a nasal voice wondering why he hadn't seen her, that he missed her: "Call me."

She erases the messages and takes to staring out of her window, a straggly tomato plant on the sill, an African violet yellowing at the edges of its velvety leaves. Rubs her temples, making small tight circles with her fingers, doesn't think she will be doing anything today, not seeing the point of much anymore.

I leave her swallowing aspirin with vodka, her face grimacing with the bitterness.

I find Michael enjoying a Scotch with William, sitting lazily around the garden table, as though nobody has died. They are even laughing about some joke about some girl Michael used to know. The garden is dry again, that spell of rain having cleared up. He doesn't seem to notice the leaves drooping around their stems. It's the reason I took to gardening, you always know what a plant is feeling, no way of mistaking it for something vague in the background – some subconscious desire, you could never see. I never possessed the energy to find out what all the drama of being human was about, plants always made sense to me. Either alive or on their way to dying, depending on how you treated them, no grey areas here in the garden.

170

Michael asks William how he is holding up, strange to say that, never seeing anyone falling and dumbfounded when they finally hit the floor.

Brave William said, of course he was holding up, but the nights were hard, the hardest really, the days too had their snags and ambushes, seeing that he was retired and had no place to go to where he thought he was needed. Told his brother he found it hard to distract himself, neglecting to tell him that every night he bites down hard on his fist, but the howling comes anyway.

Still, William is surprised that the days go by besides his reality, that it seems like a lifetime since it happened, but just a second ago, every hour, every minute, till he falls asleep and doesn't have to think anymore.

I'm not really listening to them; I just wanted to be here in some place still familiar to me, wondering about the other ways I could have died. Going down in flames or a brick hurtling to my head from the top of a scaffold and I just happened to be under it, in mid sip of tea during the evening news. A lethal slip in the bath, cracking my head open on the basin, the hairbrush still clinging to my brown tresses, because that is what I was doing before I didn't see that pesky sliver of soap. Any other way but the way I did. Not at the hand of some man fresh from the shadows with dirty underwear and kindness gone rancid in his chest.

Michael and William put their jackets on and head out. Michael has a twinkle in his eye and a shock of thick grey hair on his head. He had to twist William's arm, saying it would be fun, watching almost naked ladies wrap themselves around a pole. A boy's night out, large amounts of liquor, wolf whistles, swinging tassels and rhinestones.

"It could distract you," Michael said "Get out a bit, see the lights and all."

"Suppose it couldn't harm. I have felt cooped up here, miserable really. Not long though. Just to get a bit of air."

"That's a good man." Michael slaps William on the shoulder in a brotherly fashion. The house silent and me fearing the men come looking for me again, just to make sure I was well and truly dead. The way he climbs nonchalantly down those stairs, hands in his pockets, whistling, another notch up in the ranks.

Imogen rings the bell, come to see her father as he asked her too, ringing again, worries about him, where else would he be but here. She gets back into her car to call him, locking all the doors and rolling up the windows. The sound of loud lounge music in her ear. Noise. Glasses tinkling against each other, voices saying cheers.

"I am out with Michael. Just a while, dear. I had to get out." Imogen understands, of course. Starts her car, leaves.

Me and the house gone cold, saying but *I* am here.

16

MOTHER WANTED TO DRIVE, and she picked Imogen up at eleven in the morning. Her head peering over the steering wheel, sailing like a ship in her bronze Mercedes through stop signs, screeching tyres and she was sure the stop signs weren't there, must be new and nobody warns us, somebody could get killed, you know. Going on her maniacal way, straddling lanes and annoying taxi drivers. She has had her hair done, at the same salon she has been going to for fifteen years. She decided to do something different and had a purple rinse. The hairdresser asking, "Are you was sure, honey?" Mother looked at her bland brown curls and said yes, the hairdresser made light: "We could always go blue, you know?"

"I am too old for that," but old enough for this. You always see those old ladies sitting in the sun on the porches of old age homes, lavender hair glinting in the sun and balls of wool in their laps – there must be something in it, a certain grace? "Don't need purple hair to grow old gracefully, honey." Mother's head under a drying dome, hot and sweaty, not hearing her. Imogen, an affronted sound coming from her mouth on seeing Mother's hair, asking her what she had done.

"What do you mean, what have I done?" Mother pats the puffy curls at the back of her head, moves to the sides with her hands, showing it off. "Don't you like it, dear?"

"Well, it's different, Gran. Didn't think you would be doing that just yet."

"Neither did I, didn't plan to anyway, the idea just kind of sneaked up on me. Besides, nothing like having your hair done to feel a little more human."

Imogen nodded her head in agreement but not quite convinced. Mother missed a corpulent woman laden with parcels by a hair's breadth, told Imogen that people don't cross at the traffic lights anymore.

"And with a burden like that on top of it. What if it had been her baby, can't have your eyes everywhere, she is lucky I saw her in time!" Imogen's knuckles were white with fright, gripped on the handle of the passenger door, her foot pressing that invisible brake. I was relieved when they reached the nursery's gates, though calamity can still follow Mother into a parking lot.

"You know! Never a parking when you want one, the world and his dog out buying flowers, on a week day too. I thought it would be quieter; always struggle to find a trolley when it's busy, half the plants gone, always a pity." Imogen suggested coffee first before they tackled the depleted rows outside, needing something to quell her nerves from the drive.

Mother obliged and pushed her way to a shady spot under a tree before a nuclear family could take it. The husband almost said something but, seeing Mother's age and her new lavender hair, changed his mind and opted for a spot next to two manicured women smoking, the wife waving her hand pathetically in front of her face, the children chubby-cheeked and blue-eyed, wanting ice-creams.

Imogen ordered a latte, Mother an espresso,

wondering why these places are never licensed, Imogen happy that this one isn't. The waiter, in a stiff white apron and running shoes, brought their drinks and suggested the cake of the day. Mother told him that she was sweet enough, thank you.

It's beautiful still. William and I would always come here if we thought we should do something on a Sunday, tired of reading papers and milling about in dressing gowns, the day gone before we looked again. William would sip at a filter coffee, sliding a silver fork into the triangular sides of a chocolate cake slice. I liked the coffee shakes, a scone with cream, teaspoons of strawberry jam. The boot of the car smelled of soil and spearmint; pink sunset clouds got ready to hitch up their skirts and go home.

Mother asked for a glass of water. "To cleanse the liver, Imogen."

Should just give that idea up Mother, much too late for that.

Spring close on the heels of winter, I wanted so much to be there for it, picking things out for my garden going to ruin, like my Mother and daughter are doing. Imogen suggested a creeper of jasmine for the window at Mother's bedroom. Always such a lovely smell.

Trays of herbs, basil and rosemary, mustard leaves, for the cooking Mother never really does, living on her own.

Mother added bottles of poisons to her purchases. Imogen asked if she had heard of organic gardening. She hadn't, said she wanted to make sure the blight or bug was dead. Another African violet for Imogen, to brighten up that dreary sill. A miniature cactus, spiked with thorns, the memory of drought under its skin.

All the roses sold out, a surplus of Agapanthus.

"I got my hair rinsed, Imogen. Don't have to match with the flowers too!"

The trolley rattled over stones, back to the car, Mother's roomy boot filled to capacity. "Some good planting here, dear; my hands can't wait."

At Mother's house, the din of the traffic and near death experiences behind them, the wind calm, the sun warm on their heads, a perfect day for planting. Soil on their fingers, forks digging small holes, hands patting the soil down. Water.

"Adriana, she never had much time for a garden, never knew what to do with a patch of ground that only took up a few paces. She knew what to do with a field, a field you could stride in, get lost in even." Mother talked to Imogen with no point in mind, digging up her memories. "Strong as an ox till she passed on, carrying me on her shoulders, and I thought the entire world existed there, that I could see the end of it high up on her shoulders. Funny what you think as a child, isn't Imogen? The world soon coming around telling you it's different, more different than you ever imagined. That little life you had planned sitting there, the way you dreamed it with the sun turning around your head, disappearing as you think it. I never planned much of any of this. I had a better idea that never came to fruition. Sad thing is, I can never find the point at which it got lost, I can't go back sitting on her shoulders, marking every place with my eyes that I had been, making sure I wouldn't pass them again when I recognized them in the distance."

Imogen, when her hair got in the way, tied it up

with a yellow band she keeps around her wrist. She agreed that regret was, well, pointless.

"I think those were the best times for me, at the farm, idyllic really. What child wouldn't be happy in such a place? Always something to discover and enough room to do it in."

Imogen couldn't picture Mother as a child, all fantasy and fairy tales in her head, especially with her now lavender hair shimmering in the sun, the wrinkled folds in her neck, the liver spots on her hands and her daughter gone.

She couldn't imagine herself as a child, not sure if she had ever been one; always looking at me surprised when I told her some story. The tantrums she would throw in a supermarket, wanting something I wouldn't get her, or punishing her dolls when they were naughty, giving them sharp smacks on their plastic bums. No, Imogen didn't remember and found it harder to believe. You are there and then you are here, not knowing the gap you crossed or fell through.

"We were all cut up when Father Wilson passed on, never a kinder man to be found, Imogen. Adriana had turned to him in the morning, as she had done for the past thirty years and he was still. He looked as if he was sleeping, his face bearing no signs of what came and took him in the night as Adriana slept next to him, his body just as she had remembered it when she fell asleep curled behind him, as if it could still move towards her and wrap her up and talk about brewing a pot of coffee, strong and black as she liked it, with one spoonful of sugar. Adriana turned on her side away from her dead lover, her dearest friend. She watched the sun filtering through lace curtains, their breeches draped over a wooden chair that he had been meaning to sand down and oil; the walls, the mirror she never looked in, the room perfectly inert – gentle – watching him laugh on the insides of her eyes, that wild sky turning, her hands in his hair. It's the intimate details that break us and Adriana put her hands to her mouth, tried to cover her face best she could but her loss kept on finding her.

"Adriana did not stop crying for a month, lying in her bed, Father Wilson lying in that soft clearing, the tree with the needled leaves grown taller, casting spindly shadows over wild veld flowers.

Hannah thought Adriana would never get up again, that all her history had finally come to rest and curdle in her breast, the exhaustion she kept in the distance, finding her limbs and weakening her resolve. Hannah, me at her side, kept a hand on things best she could while Adriana sobbed relentlessly. The sterile bull, never meaning to pull a plough, his feelings offended, dug his hooves in and refused to pull no matter how hard Hannah and I pushed. Hannah cursing her mother's stubbornness, never modernizing with machines, saying, 'I can't feel what a machine is thinking, can't feel the earth and the furrows I am meant to be making. Me and the bull, we work together, its symbiotic, Hannah.' Well, Hannah called it madness. 'Why work so hard when you don't need to?' Hannah glared at Adriana, some of the precocious child still in her. 'It's just how I am, Hannah, and how the fields are.'

"Me and Mother could never figure out why the bull ignored us but pulled for all he was worth when Adriana got behind the plough. 'Maybe she has a way, Angela, a touch we will never know about. Dumb insufferable bull.' Hannah flounced off, her hand pulling at mine, marching to the slanting house, determined to get Adriana out of bed, by force if she had to.

"Adriana didn't hear any of Hannah's words about Stefan worked to the bone, and there was me to look after and they couldn't be in every place at one time and that they all missed Father Wilson, but life had to go on, didn't it? Hannah tugged and pulled at Adriana's arms that fell down slack again when she let go, realized she wasn't going to get anywhere. Adriana faced the wall again, told Hannah to leave her be, that she would know the time when to get up again. "Not everything works in seasons and rhythms. We can't predict or foresee everything, Mother. Some things can take over and never leave!" Hannah still tried to move her mother to anywhere but where she was.

"I would walk quietly at my grandmother's side, look at her hard and gentle face reddened with tears, and I was afraid, her eyes harboured a sorrow I had never seen before. I wondered what was wrong with Gran. Would she lift me up on her shoulders and was Gran going to die? 'No, Angela. Not yet.'

"The weather was foul, blistering cold that made my teeth chatter and my jaw clench, autumn was sent packing and took its sepia leaves and soft sun with it, in a suitcase made of birch and lichen, water running over stones and who you might have kissed there, a piece of driftwood a cousin brought from the coast because you'd never seen the sea. Everything covered in frost and puddles of water filming over with ice, the animals taking strain, huddling closer and closer."

They had gone inside, the wind had picked up, trying to huff and puff the winter away, still thick and grey around Table Mountain. Mother took out gold-rimmed shot glasses. Usually, when she was drinking alone, she wouldn't care so much what she would drink out of, but with Imogen it was different, she lent a certain elegance to the occasion.

Mother sipped delicately. Patted a crease in her skirt. "She got up eventually, the tears drying up as suddenly as they had started. The sun, incongruous and warm, made its same dust-filtered sweep across the room. Adriana drew herself a bath, rubbed dried lavender between her fingers, letting it fall into the steaming water. Her body felt older, as though it had run a long and impossible distance. She submerged herself into the water lapping around her sides, her long hair seeping like blood around her.

"Adriana rested there, contemplating the world without Father Wilson, blinking her eyes, adjusting her vision. She was relieved that the tears had stayed gone. She thought of her mother burying things in the riverbeds when they had gotten wind of the war: their best crockery, sealed trunks with folds of good lace, coins; thinking it would still be there when it was over, that they would be back to dig it out again. Adriana had her hands in the muddy clay, her mother had told her to dig faster, their boots sunken in the mud, skirts soiled, her mother's jaw set tight against the bare trees, Adriana remembered. They took them away, her mother and her, her little sister, her father was already off fighting. They didn't know where they were going, on bumpy carts, their house a vanishing spot on the burning horizon.

"The conditions they were taken to were more appalling than you can imagine, Imogen. Adriana's mother, suffering from a weak constitution, succumbed to disease, her little sister from exhaustion and starvation. Adriana figuring that they died because they never thought it could happen, the horror of it. That it was better to leave than stay. Adriana kept her resolve, measuring out her days, whatever they still meant, she was still breathing. When it was over and the sun blinded her eyes and her bones prodded through her skin, thinking that love had been the only strength that kept her alive and she wasn't good enough for him, because she was pregnant from another man.

"Her mother and sister were dead, her father returned with a missing limb and a savage look in his eyes to the charred ground where the house once stood, driven mad with grief. Adriana had watched him run into the lilting hills and he never returned. She got out of the bath, towelled herself dry, put on her breeches which were draped over the chair, donned her veld hat, strode out into the fields, scattering chickens, the tall grasses cheering."

Imogen refused Mother's shaking hand teetering on the edges of pathological alcoholism, and she was grateful that her head wasn't swimming. She worried about William and his night of debauchery most certainly making trouble in his head and stomach. Mother understood. "Should be looking in on your father, don't know how he is managing," she tells Imogen she enjoys their stories, that they are important. "You have to know where you come from, dear, before I can't tell it to you how I remember it."

Imogen knew she should be working, meeting those

181

deadlines, but she couldn't find it in herself to see how it could help her sense of dread, that the middle was gone and nothing could bring it back again.

Me, I am a road nobody passes through, as my daughter kisses my mother goodbye. The people that used to live there are dead from influenza or from their own hands, turning against each other till none were left. An old wooden windmill: its wafer arms turning sullenly against a mustard sky, ribs protruding from the shoulder, a long-dead animal, wind screaming through the spaces the vultures made. Tumbling weeds coming to rest at the trunks of thorn trees, swirls of dust, gritty in the eyes, the well, long dried up. Boarded windows and candles blown out. It is lonelier in the dark. The headlights dip and rise in the distance, trying to finding another route, the wife in the car saying to her husband, "Anywhere but through there."

William curses his brother, tells Imogen that he now knows why he sees him so infrequently. "You would swear he was twenty years old, dear. I have never had such a headache; just about overdosed on aspirin."

"Need something greasy to mop it all up, Dad. Have you never had a hangover?"

"Well, not like this. Lining up shots with lewd names for me. Really, Imogen, it was a nightmare and he wouldn't take no for an answer. Determined to show me a good time! I hope he is feeling just as crap as I am, that brother of mine, telling me life is too short. Like I don't know?"

I could picture the scene. Foreign women gyrating on their laps, sliding down poles, balding men sweaty and playing in their pockets, putting notes into sequined G-strings, between ample cleavages.

William, shy and chivalrous, rather wanting to talk, "How does it feel to have all these men gawking at you?" The women were as hard as nails and thought he must have a limp dick.

Imogen makes her father a mug of tea and gives him slices of toast smeared with butter. He swallows heavily and with much exaggerated effort. "I miss your mother, dear. Miss her so much it feels like missing alone could make me disappear, or kill me on the spot."

Imogen is busily folding some of his trousers back into the cupboard, glancing at my clothes still hanging there, deciding that the trousers and other items of clothing lying around need a wash rather, putting them in the washing machine on the hot cycle. Ordering papers into neat piles, throwing away foil containers with half-eaten dinners, scraping dried instant oats off bowls, putting cups into the sink, up to her arms in soap suds. Drying it all to a clinical shine.

William calls from his revolving room that, "It isn't necessary to wash anything, dear." He has called someone to help around the house. "She's coming tomorrow, rather come and talk."

William had founded that card in his pocket, overwhelmed by the burden of keeping order.

Imogen is annoyed that her sleeves have got wet, and her hands still itching to dust and mop, and drag that old Hoover out. Sitting next to him on the bed, her arms folded. "Heard anything from the police, Dad?" Well if they were going to talk, may as well begin at trying not to be complacent.

William unable to control a laugh, hollow and tired from his lungs. "The police. Are you serious? I doubt we will ever hear from them again."

"But nothing is happening, Dad. This crime cannot escape unpunished, can it?

"Worse things happen, don't they?"

Imogen is sure William is still drunk and not a word of sense is coming from his lips. "What do you mean by that, Dad?"

"Just what I mean. I feel so wretched, Imogen. Why all these questions?"

"Well, what did you mean?"

"That the despicable nature of your mother's passing is commonplace, that something must be terribly wrong here, even more frightening and repugnant than the symptoms, if we can become used to it and so apathetic as though life has lost all value and importance!" William holds his head in one hand, and sips gingerly at his tea with the other.

"So, are we just going to wait till they get around to doing something?"

"They found the car. That is a start, isn't it?"

"They did? Where is it then?"

"I told them they could keep it. Well, I wanted to say they could shove it, but decided not to."

"Nothing else, no leads, nothing from the fingerprints?"

"Guess not. The police don't really tell you anything, Imogen. Leave you to figure out the case if they could, all secrets and forms and ineffectiveness."

"I don't think you are being bold enough, Dad. Do something; get mad if you have to."

"Yes, dear. In the morning I will wake up and

get mad at them; I just want to sleep now." Imogen, knowing when it is pointless, takes the empty mug from her father, the remaining slice of toast, starts the process of washing all over again. Tackling the bathroom next, scrubbing with ammonia, burning her lungs, coughing, scrubbing, rinsing with a hysterical determination to see that she had made something look better, just for a while. Sitting spent and dazed on the couch, the cookie jar in her hands. You really should be getting rid of me, no use in hanging on, is there?

Putting me back on my spot on the shelf, so that I have a view of the Bougainvillea.

Crying herself into a fitful sleep, dreaming of shadows and barrels of guns glinting, laughing, teeth sharpened to fine points and yellow eyes staring, a man coming up close to her, hissing in her ear, his peak cap pulled over permed lavender hair, getting out of her car small enough to carry under her arm, Tannie Piep, doing backstroke in a giant red-centred cookie.

17

THERE WAS ONCE A MAN with three heads, and those he ruled over could never quite understand him. Where he came from nobody knew. Some said he came from deep in the earth, forged from a hot molten fire. Some looked to the sky and said, yes, that is where he came from. His mind grinding like the wheels of a machine, the tiny intricate cogs, spinning webs and spinning lies with relentless aggression.

The three heads spoke of different things but always in agreement with each other. One head, with dead fish eyes, came to a land and said, "We must grow a garden. We need vegetables for the sailors, sick and afflicted with scurvy. We must establish ourselves. We need some hands, slave hands, because we don't want to do the establishing ourselves, yes, that is what we will do." And his minions saying yes too, running to find those slaves, bringing them in ships from homes and hills and rivers they would never see again.

"We will punish them if they disobey us. We will break their bodies on wheels and flog them. Yes, we will leave sore raised welts in their backs, let them run on a treadmill, impale them through the anus, that must hurt, but they are only slaves and don't feel, just like the animals, leave them to die, the birds pecking at their eyes. Work them in the fields till they die."

All stood gormlessly below nodding their heads,

bloodthirsty and violent, their fists itching for something to do after the wives had made them their evening meal.

"Yes, because I say so, because I have a white skin and I have been known to do anything." The slaves turning on themselves, becoming accustomed to the atrocities they have to endure, mirroring their master's inhumane behaviour.

"So it is and so it shall be," and he smiled, pleased with what he had created.

Another head lifting its eyes up into the heavens saying the Bible told him so, a beatific, self-righteous expression on his face. Man over the animals and over the women. The sorry souls below stunned into obedience on account of all that misery and atrocity, nodding their heads. Because they are not thought of as men, they will wield their strength elsewhere. "Keep her bound, keep her silent, keep her sore, just like us."

The man with the three heads not noticing or hearing the chaos below him, the broken families and broken people, the men with the whips growing more savage with each flogging, neither knowing why, neither knowing who or what they might be. Just following orders, just doing what everyone else is doing, just internalizing our many deaths. The man with the three heads praying on Sundays, preaching God and love.

Another, writing division and persecution into law, putting a thought through pen to paper, and telling different faces that some will be free and others won't be.

"But the ones who are not free will build for us, will take the gold and the diamonds out from our mines, will keep our homes and gardens clean, will do the work we are too good for." Cooking up plans over beers, rubbing his white chin with a fat hand in his little hideaway room, thinking up things, conjuring hell in a suburban home and the son tinkering on his Chevy in the garage. The smell of boerewors sizzling on coals, the NG Kerk sermonizing and sanctifying hate, the language of the oppressor forced down our throats in every classroom, and wherever we move, even in the privacy of our homes. *Die Stem* every evening on television when the dubbed programmes had come to an end, the presidential address, a goodnight lullaby, the man's finger shaking with zeal. Spewing garbage from his mouth, and not enough of us recoiling from the stench of his words, happy that Prudence was hushing the baby with township songs, happy that Samuel was in the garden raking up those pesky leaves.

The heads below nodding again, though some knowing better thought there was something very wrong with this. But the man with the three heads paid no mind to the violent protestations, creating a police state rather, to enforce those laws in a land where we could hate even more. His henchmen having signed those laws with deplorable hands, passing them, letting them exist and thrive. Our world got smaller, the weather the same, a blank grey sky where nothing sang, where nothing could be beautifully different. Strange how we all baled towards the rainbow when it came, drawn out from a magician's sleeve, tumbling out of our stifled walls, running to it as if we hadn't been allowed to draw air into our lungs for centuries, the tightening noose loosened from our throats, because one man spoke of kindness, spoke of love for once.

Where the man with the three heads went to nobody

knows, nor how he managed for so long to destroy us. We are all still looking for him, wanting to drive a stake through his worm-eaten heart, aiming anywhere.

Me, I was old enough to do something, wasn't I? Make that bit of difference, join the liberals, if I looked hard enough I could have. Grown used to the unnatural normalcy of the days and the years, as though I was drugged, waiting to wake up from a long and dreamless sleep, not blinking much anymore at the whites only signs, not even hearing the miserable words before the testing pattern on television, turning it off or yawning for oxygen – filled with such hate at the words tying my hands and cutting the voice from my throat. It always gave me indigestion, William saying I was such a sensitive one, and shouldn't get so worked up about it: "Something we cannot change, dear."

Imogen wasn't old enough to go marching and burning that old flag and that rainbow coming just in time for her, left with the mess us older ones have made.

Imogen, woken up by her father, her head still stuck in nightmares, the metal stairs tugging at her arm, steel catching the fabric of her shirt, turning and turning like a winch would, constricting her breath, making her eyes bulge, yelping herself to consciousness. Discovering the blanket twisted around herself, her father pulling at her sleeve.

"Meet Griet," he says, smiling at her, a maniacal expression in his eyes, a tight coil on the brink of snapping again. Griet looking like she had just blown in straight from the Kalahari, picking up a housecoat on her way, a *doek* wrapped around her head, a print of orange roses in full bloom. Hard lines of drinking furrowed in her face. Our infamous *dop* system coming back to bite her. Imogen extricates her hand from the blanket hell-bent on strangling her and shakes Griet's hand, papery and thin, apologizes, saying that she is not usually like this.

Embroidered words in yellow thread on the lapel of Griet's pink housecoat: "Busy Hands." Imogen trying to focus on the mélange of colours, rubs her eyes to adjust her vision, still sore from the night's crying.

Griet smiles and asks William where the cleaning products are. He opens cabinet doors one after the other. "I know they are here somewhere, Griet."

"Under the sink, Dad." Imogen craws back under her blanket, not ready to get up just yet.

Griet thinks that William manages very well without help. Everything so deceptively clean and shiny.

"My daughter, last night, she got it in her to scrub everything, I tried to stop her, but there is no messing with her when she is wielding a mop."

Griet, an unimpressed expression on her face, starts filling the sink for dishes that will surely come. William makes coffee, not wanting to get into Griet's way. She is finding things to do, dusting with a yellow cloth that fine film of dust that collects overnight and settles over everything again.

The door bell rings. Mrs Watson stands on the sidewalk at the gate, another plate covered in foil in her hand.

William tells her he has just put a pot of coffee on to brew and invites her in.

Mrs Watson almost sitting herself down on Imogen's

legs, pushing the blanket blindly to the side, "Oh, I didn't see you here, dear. Shift up, won't you?"

Imogen, abandoning the thought of a lie-in sits up, pulling the blanket around her shoulders.

"Brought you some pumpkin fritters, William, and for you Imogen. The more the merrier."

The sound of Griet pulling out the Hoover from the cupboard, Mrs Watson babbling on endlessly. "Got those fritters just like my mother made them, quite proud even if I say so myself."

William pours coffee in cups, takes out plates, asks Griet to join them for a spot of breakfast. Mrs Watson does not know what to make of Griet; William introduces her like she was one of *them*. An old friend, eating her pumpkin fritters and drinking out of the same cups and eating off the same plates, wondering where to sit. Imogen watching old fossil Watson, a delicious smile between sips of coffee.

William asks Griet where she lives. She puts her hand under her *doek,* neatening hair that hasn't come astray.

"The Cape Flats, Mr Jenkins," taking a bite of pumpkin fritter. "My Ma, she used to make these too, on Sundays, she used to work in the vineyards."

Mrs Watson jumps in, sending Griet's words scattering. Griet looking into her lap, brushing off a crumb, going silent again. "William, I think I have a hand on those aphids, got a good bug spray, watched them dropping to the ground dead, pesky little blights messing around with an old woman's roses!"

Imogen trying hard to stifle a laugh in her coffee cup. Griet clearing the plates, thanking old Watson for the fritters, William for the coffee, smiling at Imogen, her hands busy in the soapy hot water.

"Well, William, I best be going, have a hedge I thought of trimming, though I don't know with these old hands anymore, and it so hard to find reliable and trustworthy help these days."

Griet turning up the volume a little in her sink of water. William grinning sheepishly at Imogen. Rolling his eyes. Mrs Watson taking her plate back clean and dried, walking to the door with stiff arthritic legs, commenting on the lovely day, can even hear the birds singing, almost placing her bulky flat heeled shoe into shit on the sidewalk, saying to no one that the neighbourhood is going to the dogs.

Griet lugging the Hoover upstairs, looking too old to be lugging anything. The sound of vacuuming, furniture moved and scraped across the wooden floors, a black hole where strolls through the parks and Sunday drives and baking cakes and getting up and going to sleep disappear – all the inconsequential memories I strung between stars.

William taking to the couch, suddenly weary, a yellow tinge in his face.

"Where did you find Griet, Dad?" Imogen drinking at another cup of coffee, the day not quite convincing her to do anything yet.

"From the cleaning company. The woman, Ms Claasens, gave me a number, said they helped in times of death or illness. Busy Hands, what a name, being busy for you because you couldn't care anymore."

"Kind of depressing, isn't it, Dad?"

"What isn't, when you really look at it? Besides, the owners of the company do good work, all the women are from impoverished areas, a religious set up, giving them hope and such, food on the table. Trying to make some difference in a desperate situation."

"Kind of patronizing too, that the only hope they could figure in the desperate situation was cleaning other peoples' homes. Is there ever anything else, Dad? What about something really uplifting? All just the same thing stamped and approved with a verse from the Bible."

"Imogen, it is better than doing nothing at all about it, isn't it?"

"I don't know, Dad, it all lacks the edge of invention. Walking the same done-to-death paths." Imogen never thought much of charity, churchwomen high on polyester thread, their needles clicking, cutting carrots into cubes for a hearty broth, smiling condescendingly at the hand which takes it. One single woman against all odds opening her home, trying to save all the Aids orphans, when she didn't have to, had the now dead parents thought first. A camera will zoom in on the plights of many, the walls painted cheerily in rainbow colours, dishing oats in metal bowls, making peanut butter sandwiches, changing nappies, wiping noses, singing lullabies, hoping for a change that never comes. Charities filling in the gaps where the government should be, somewhere to go, nowhere to go. Imogen thought of another name, Frantic Hands, never having had much time for euphemism.

Griet lugging the Hoover down again, arms like toothpicks. Imogen going to help her.

"*Ag*, its alright, lovey, thank you." Plugging it in the socket behind the television, William casually lifting up his legs as she vacuums around him, paging through one of my décor magazines.

"Your mother loved these, always wanting to pretty something up. 'How to bring the life back into your scatter cushions.' 'A new artistic way of letting curtains fall.' 'Gardening to the phases of the moon.' Things like that. She used to read them aloud to me, when we were in bed, I would nod off, Imogen, not because of the content, just the sound of your mother reading to me, as if she was reading a love story, she made even paint sound sensual. I miss that." William putting the magazine away, folding it up into a tight telescopic roll.

Imogen can't imagine me being sensual, always cold and removed, strangely detached. I never thought I described the glossy pages that way either, always surprising how our lovers see and perceive us.

The drone of the Hoover switched off, a mop and a bucket of soapy water, the wet mop slapped against the floor, gliding across the tiles as if it is waltzing, hands wringing out the scummy water, again and again till the floor shines. William making a list for a shopping errand, the trembling in his hand worsening, handing it to Griet with a wad of money, William not knowing the price of groceries. Griet neatening her hair, dusting the front of her housecoat before making her way up the street.

I remember my adolescent bedroom, psychedelic posters on the wall, dried and crushed marijuana leaves and free love, trying to roll a joint, and I knew even then that there was always a price to pay for love. Bob Dylan and Janis Joplin and Melanie's arms around me, the smell of danger and escape and possible happy-ever-afters. I was almost sixteen, certainly shy and awkward and me and Melanie had been friends since nursery school. Wondering why we wanted to hold each other, why we wanted to draw each other nearer. Kiss even, my stomach queasy with nerves or love.

Melanie was always cool, and I knew nothing about cool, it was another planet for me. Whatever I tried never looked right, the skirt would bunch, the shirt wouldn't fall properly, my hair wouldn't iron straight, even my jeans wouldn't wear out in the right places. Melanie was considered to be one of the wild girls who possessed dubious morals and I loved her all the more for it. I wanted to be a wild girl, not a straight-laced and tight-lipped girl that no one ever invited to Saturday parties. I wanted to be succulent like a juicy exotic fruit, red pouting lips that were always moist with lip gloss, salacious and, yes, reclining somewhere in a resplendent room with bright feathers around my neck. Instead we wore jeans flared at the bottoms, the threads tatty, embroidered with peace signs at the pockets. Tie-dyed T-shirts. A penchant for underage drinking and smoking. We decided not to shave our underarms and declined the boerewors at the Sunday braai, waxing lyrical about the energy of the humble lentil. We were inseparable, even took the same classes at school so we never had to be apart, our scuffed school shoes touching as we pretended to listen to the teacher drone on about reproductive system of the earthworm.

Then Mother discovered us. We were careful with our afternoon homework sessions, having explored beyond kissing in my bedroom, which Mother quickly turned into a den of obscenity. Obscenity for mother was many things. The snails in her gardens, the pigeons chasing the robins away, Mrs Van Niekerk over the street always receiving a man at her door that wasn't her husband, a cake she baked that didn't come out right, flat in the middle, folding suggestively in places. "Look at it, Sarah, what does it remind you of? My Lord we can't eat this. We should serve it to your father, tell him I made something special for him on account of all the bad days, he always wanted me handed to him on a plate!"

Bob Dylan croaking through his last verse of "Blowin' in the Wind", Mother's hand neglecting to knock at the door, standing aghast in the open door way, the plate of sandwiches in her hand trembling. She must have caught sight of Melanie's daisy tattoo – intricately pricked into the left globe of her luxurious behind – her bare back, her right breast cupped in my hand, my knobby knees trying to get back under the covers. Mother's face takes on the hue of the beetroot she liked to boil up sometimes when she wasn't feeling imaginative ("Looks like the river Nile in this pot, Sarah, think there will be any bleeding tonight, can never tell can we?")

Mother's mouth is moving like my goldfish in its bowl near the window, but no words are coming out of her. I think time has stopped or slowed down considerably. This is a very long and drawn-out humiliation. I don't know if I have covered myself up or if I am still exposed. Mother has left, back through the way she came, closing the door very quietly behind her. Melanie swearing like a sailor, her face a troubling shade of puce. Her hands fumbling for her jeans and her T-shirt, tripping, shoving her feet into espadrilles.

"I better go," she said. How would she manage

to go with Mother stalking in the house, waiting to pounce on her, demanding explanations, or worse still, Mother working herself up to a wail, cursing her luck, banging her head on the kitchen counter, flattening that new tight perm?

Melanie abseiling down the trellis, trying to swing her way around the concrete birdbath, missing and breaking it into two neat pieces, clean down the middle. More cursing, rubbing her ankle, waving at me from below, apologizing for breaking Mother's birdbath, she always watched out of the window, saying, "Birds always look so happy, Sarah."

Melanie running to the gate, lifting the latch, disappearing down the avenue of trees, the smell of patchouli still on my fingers, on my skin.

I pulled the covers around me, dreading any altercation, the slightest hints of a confrontation that didn't come till I couldn't hold a pee anymore and had to venture out to the bathroom, walking into Mother sorting out the linen cupboard; only Mother can fold towels noisily.

"Sarah, you come back here." I thought I could escape, lock myself into the white sterile bathroom and ponder my existence from now on.

"I need to pee, Ma."

"You will be doing nothing of the sort now. All this time, Sarah, right under my nose, with that loose girl, and smoking those drugs too!"

"She isn't loose, Ma. Even if she was, so what?"

"So what? What do you mean 'so what'? We have a name to keep clean, we have our pride, Sarah, and here you are doing God knows what in that den of inequity of yours. Getting up to obscenities, unnatural obscenities. If it was some dull boy with his trousers too short and lanky arms I could understand, Sarah, could send him packing, I could find the right words. I knew she was no good."

"But how could you know, Ma? We were always friends, since we were little, she was good enough then!"

"Well, times change, Sarah, the worm turns and I forbid you to see her."

"We go to the same school, take the same classes, how can I not see her?"

"We will change your school, then, or your classes, or something!"

"You can't do that, not now when I am two years away from being done."

"I am very angry now, Sarah, and I can't think of a word of sense to say to you. You just cannot bring that girl here anymore, do you understand. If your father hears of this, all hell will break loose, you know that. This never happened, I didn't see it, you didn't do it. We will forget about it, Sarah." Mother folds the towels in precise edges, stacking them flush with the shelf.

"But I can't forget about it, Ma. What if it's who I am? I love Melanie."

Mother coming right up to my face, her lips tight and her teeth clenching, violence in her eyes. "You are not like that Sarah, that is not you and you know nothing of love. You get rid of it now, do you hear?"

I, not possessing the same stubbornness and strong will as my grandmother, Hannah, nodded obediently, went to the bathroom to lose those sandwiches I never ate.

The arms of our striped blazers still touched in class, thinking Mother couldn't spy on us here, pulling each other into dark shadowy corners, where teachers were never known to walk, making ourselves dizzy with illicit kisses. Then *she* found that dull boy with trousers too short and lanky arms and, "We were just friends, you know, we can still be friends, can't we?"

Having given Mother the impression that I had strangled love, I couldn't tell her about my wounded pride, nor my heart that felt broken to me.

"So sullen these days you are, Sarah. Cheer yourself up, no good being gloomy."

I went back to being uncool, letting a boy paw at my breasts. Trying to feel something but never really managing, not even the applicable sigh at the end you read in books for housewives. Don't bother him with talk about your day, your interests are unimportant in comparison, have his drink ready, if he is wanting congress make yourself pretty first, a sigh at the end will suffice. Never let him see you without make-up.

William was different, tried to astound me, bent over backwards to have me at his side, took his time, even spoke to me. I loved him the way a sister loves her brother, but in time I could learn how to be attracted to him, to feel that queasiness every time he entered a room. Mother was overjoyed that I was courting a handsome young man. "And studying engineering too. You can't go wrong, Sarah, with an engineer. He will give you a good life." I wanted my own life too, something I spun in my head, the words not quite remembered, but Mother looked so happy. I could look happy too.

Then there was Emily. I wanted to broaden that ever-shrinking horizon and signed up for a flower-arranging course. Thirteen years into a marriage that was comfortable and had its habits and routines and occasional earthquakes.

I was fascinated by her. We got on from the beginning, sharing the same humour, reading similar books, liking the same music drawn from a dusty sleeve. Not for Emily the stiff and tortured arrangements of women who could never groan between the sheets. Her flowers lay lazily in their green oasis islands, draped over each other; their leaves open hands inviting me to some place I had forgotten.

The instructor, we guessed in her early seventies, in a cardigan, a brooch pinned close to her clavicle bone, a hint of rose perfume on her powdered cheeks, saying Emily's arrangements lacked form. "There is no scale, dearie, you need some shape, it's all a mishmash, unpleasing to the observer's eye. Follow Sarah's example of uniformity." Emily unravelling the neatness in me, taking me to uncharted places, yet, yes, I recognize this. I know your hands making me fall in ways I tried so hard not to want.

I remember pulling away from William when he tried to touch me, seduce me. I had a headache, the dinner too rich had made me sluggish and uncomfortable. "All that bouncing around, dear, it won't sit well with me now." William putting his arms around me instead, giving up the idea of sex, me waking up happy because I would be seeing her in that room with the indigo sky.

Out for coffee again with Emily. William at work, what would he know? Though I hated the deceit all the same.

William worried about my stomach and my recurrent headaches, worried that I didn't find him appealing anymore. "It isn't you, love, just feel a little peculiar lately," though I had never felt so happy, nor so in love. A year of lies and falling irretrievably into a rhythm I had always missed.

William threatening an affair with his secretary who always brings him something sweet from her lunch break, or throwing himself at prostitutes because he never got any anymore "Why, when I love you so much, when you love me so much? Don't you? The truth will out, Sarah."

"Yes and no, William. It's Emily, it's her that I am in love with. I tried to ignore it, further back than you think, but I can't. It's who I am, William!"

William quiet and speechless for a long uncomfortable time, working out the words in his head. "I can't lose you, Sarah. I love you too much. Where the idea of self preservation is lost, against all reason and rationality, is how I love you, you know that don't you? She cannot love you like I do."

"How do you know how she loves me William? How can you can sit there and assume the love I need?"

"What about Imogen, your daughter?"

"Don't bring her into this; this is our problem not hers."

"No, Sarah, it is your problem that you have now involved us in."

"She doesn't need to know, no one does."

"You're right, I will never live it down, will be the laughing stock of the office, my wife run off with another woman!"

You could say I couldn't see the point in fighting.

Mother would never forgive me, neither would William. Imogen would have understood; I know she would have. I was married, a wife and mother, who was I trying to fool, trying to live my life over the way I wanted to, when it was too late?

"It's just a phase," William said. "It will work itself out, we could work it out, for better or for worse," he said.

So it was for the worse for a long time, me having explained to Emily that I couldn't see her anymore, her anger, her tears, her back turned against me though I still wanted her, never stopped wanting her, mourning her like she had died and William trying to be cheerful, trying to get me interested in things again, trying to hide the hurt and betrayed expression from his eyes. You could say I crawled back up again, from whatever cliff I had thrown myself off of, thinking I was flying. Back to the magazines, licking my fingers before turning the glossy pages, back to the baking and standing in shopping aisles, listening to Imogen talk about school between putting pots on to boil, smiling sweetly at William when he walked through the door, knowing that there was never any forgetting that another's hands could burn me so.

Imogen left her father in the capable hands of Griet, cooking him a square dinner, potatoes, a steak, long green beans, declining the invitation to join. The laptop screen flickered in the hazy late afternoon, Mother's little helper clear and smooth in a long glass. A rolled joint waiting to be lit. I never knew Imogen, well I knew, why not, whatever helps, love. Your mother did that many times, even the harder things if you can believe it, in another life.

18

THERE IS A BACKDROP, an idea, of humanity that we all aspire to.

Strange to be talking about humanity in such times, human rights, humanitarianism, human rights violations. What does it all mean, Imogen? We are as we are, capable of anything, anything that goes beyond the boundaries of mere imagination, see how far you can stretch. We violate the idea of humanity all the time, justifying it with some burning cause or other, feeling offended and insulted, slighted, baring our teeth whenever the opportunity arises and if one doesn't present itself we create one. The world trying to develop a modicum of behaviour, a basic decency towards others, but there isn't much point to it is there, really? The world answering back, thinking up new and more vicious ways of setting back the clock, the perpetrators slipping through legal loopholes. Anything can be written on paper, never means the words will be respected or honoured. There is a responsibility in democracy, Imogen, a give and take, it needs room to move, it needs to understand its freedom and the freedom of others, the autonomous dignity of another. It needs to know the boundaries pegged in the grounds of the constitution.

We have known no other language in this country,

steeped in disrespect and violence, we spew the same words, fight the same fights, we never leave from here and never get it right. What a waste it is, Imogen, what a sad and terrible discourtesy to those who fought long and hard to free us all.

Imogen, not seeing hope either, fails to produce another sentence.

She phones the man with the nasal voice instead, getting his answering machine. She had wanted to see a film or go out for a coffee somewhere, but she said nothing after the voice on the other end said, "You know what to do after the beep."

19

Esmeralda walks to school, shoulders hunched, shoes kicking at occasional stones. The air is crisp with undertones of garbage rotting in the morning sun. Walking past more nondescript blocks of flats and staircases just like hers, women with curlers in their hair, bending down to hang up sheets, wire fences, plastic packets caught in their hands. She didn't feel like going, would rather hang around with the boys getting high or stay asleep.

Her mother shakes her fists at her, telling her she is ruining her life and, looking around her, it was already ruined before she even started, but her mother doesn't see that, telling her all the time that she could make good if she believed enough. But Esmeralda doesn't believe in anything now that her brothers are dead, all caught up in gangs like most of the boys and men in her neighbourhood are and everyone knowing about it. Her mother is relying on her, she figures, to make it to some other place, far away from here. She knows she shouldn't feel so tired, not even seventeen yet, knows she shouldn't feel so hopeless but she does, doesn't see the point in smiling or trying when it never stops, always something to be sad over, something she has to escape in her head.

She used to like school in the very beginning, she could imagine sometimes she was somewhere else, that she had already grown up and had a pretty house and a handsome husband who loved only her and she had a career, something important, she just didn't know what yet. Then that teacher liking her, cornering her after school or before, always waiting for her, telling her she was pretty, sometimes not even that, just taking her as though it was normal, as though he was allowed to, because he was the teacher. She knew of other girls like her, ones that were gang raped in toilet cubicles or in the fields, the rapists looking for a virgin cure for Aids, like all the boys around her think, or just for the fun of it. They never talked much about it, having already grown hard and used to it, taking the money teachers might offer them in exchange for a fuck.

Her mother just about kicking her out of the house when she found out she was pregnant, asking if it was that no good gangsta boy she hung around with who had done this. She had said no, but couldn't tell her mother who had done it to her. Her mother, thinking she was lying about the boy, stormed out of the house and took a stick to him anyway. Of course, he didn't want to know Esmeralda after that, nobody wanted to know Esmeralda after that, not even the teacher, looking a little nervous in class now that her belly was swelling, his eyes and his hands looking elsewhere.

William works up the courage to phone the police; he shifts on his feet, asks for Inspector Fredericks. Inspector Fredericks is not available. William is comforted by the fact that he can't get hold of him. They must be riding the waves of crime in a superhero cape, a busy man, a busy woman having not closed their eyes to sleep in years. He tries another number and gets his voice-mail, annoyance fizzes in William's throat and he slams the phone down. He will call later, won't he?

Griet is in the kitchen washing the supper dishes that he never got to, asks if he wants coffee.

William is trying to stay off the liquor, but recognizes the opportune moment to give in and resist, nods his head. He is glad he called and they sent Griet, he doesn't feel so lonely in the house, so large and cavernous without me, though Imogen seems to be making the couch her second home. He doesn't mind that either. He misses her today, said she had to work, had to go and type something before she forgot how to think or remember anything, put words into a coherent sentence.

William doesn't need to remember anything really, being retired, can fill his days with pottering around and do it all over again the next day. Griet brings him a steamy mug of coffee. He says thank you, doesn't know what she does but she makes the best coffee, asks what her secret is.

"*Ag*, I just make it, no secret." Going back to the kitchen, wiping down cabinets that don't need wiping down.

William puts the mug down and reaches for my ashes, holds the cookie jar in his hands, lifts the lid carefully, not sure if he is disturbing me or not, or being disrespectful to the dead. Just ashes, William, nothing more and I still move through the same atmosphere as you. His mind is restless today, turning like a cog, threatening vengeance. If he finds them they are going to wish they were dead instead. He is talking to me, sometimes aloud, Griet saying, "Excuse me? I didn't hear."

"Just talking to someone else," he responds. Seeing no one else there, Griet looks worried. He wonders if he could kill to balance the scales, an eye for an eye, what it would really take to end another's life, where he would have to go inside his head to make it real. He doesn't know where he would have to go and knows he could never do it, despite his anger, his abject sorrow, his grief. What if it was done to you again and again William, would you find hell enough in your head to pull the trigger, lunge with that knife and would you walk or run away afterwards? What would happen to you if you were backed into a corner so tight all you could do was turn in small circles where you stood? Would you break through to another rank and dark room never knowing how you got there and shocked at what you were capable of now, turning your veins to steel? "But he was such a gentle man," the disbelieving will say. "Some hinge come loose in his head and he never stopped screaming, but he was somebody's husband, somebody's father."

You couldn't hurt a fly, could you William? Isn't that why I married you, having had enough of the violence? I liked the way you looked like open fields.

He tries the inspector again. This time there is an answer at the other end. "Aah, Mr Jenkins, how are you?"

"Annoyed, thank you." William wonders if honesty will get him arrested. "Why has there been no progress on my wife's murder, Inspector? I have heard just about nothing from you, as though it happened and that's all there is to it, take those fingerprints, pack up and go home, never telling us you had no intention of ever bringing the perpetrators to book!"

"We are doing all we can, Mr Jenkins. We are short-staffed; we have little resources to make headway, to get through the backlogs. You know how it is, please try to understand." William isn't convinced, nor is he in any mood to be understanding, what with the memory of me in that chair scraping the insides of his skull.

"You think my wife gives a rat's ass about your staff shortages or your backlogs? She is dead, Inspector, and she isn't supposed to be. The least you can do is find them, or even a suspect! You are the most ineffectual, infuriating, bureaucratic bunch of people I have ever had the displeasure of having dealt with!"

"Now, Mr Jenkins, there is no need for that, I understand that you are angry and that you are under stress, but you are knocking on the wrong door."

"I suspect I am, Inspector!" William slams the receiver down, breathes hard like a steam train coming into the station. Pours that drink. Three fingers disappearing in one swallow.

He rubs his eyes, trying to erase me but I keep coming back. I won't let him sleep peacefully, he's twisting the sheets, the sheets damp, waking up from an hour or two of rest to the same images of me in his head. I won't let him eat though he tries, it all finds its way back out again somewhere in the small hours, his stomach constantly gnawing at itself, hungry, beyond empty, sated from hardly a bite. I make his head hurt, make it throb with relentless blinding pains and he tries to smile for Imogen, tries to be brave and not let on how he really feels but he feels he is losing. He doesn't see beautiful things anymore, trees once loved look sinister, their scratchy fingers clawing at his collar pulling him back, everything morphing into monsters, children's faces smiling blood, bodies walking in the streets with holes in them, faces with no eyes or no mouths, or slits exposing jagged teeth. Food writhing with maggots, the food on his plate, the food in his mouth swelling, wriggling.

"You must eat, Mr Jenkins, keep up your strength."

Waking up screaming at night, screaming with his eyes open in the clear light of day. William curled up on our bed shaking as if the temperature had suddenly dropped to below freezing and he wasn't prepared.

20

Imogen answers her ringing phone, Griet's voice is frantic, tells her that her father has gone mad, that he is breaking everything, and she had to come quickly.

I could see it coming, but I couldn't warn anybody, nor could I stop William going to where he was going, the drink in him turning his rage cold and precise, aiming at anything that was in his way. Griet hearing things breaking on the floors upstairs, the house turned upside down and inside out where he passed. She ran upstairs, calling him, a little afraid as he looked twice his size and capable of snapping trees in half like matchsticks. Trying to get a hold of him, her boss at the company telling her a little about what had happened, that she should be sensitive to that. Pushing her away, clearing the shelves and desks and tables of ornaments and papers and things that never have a place in a drawer. Griet shouting at him, thinking that if she raised her voice he would come back or realize where he is, trying to hold his arms, now flailing about helplessly, trying to soothe him but he will hear nothing of it, finding renewed anger that was crying and breaking everything at the same time. She had brought her son down once or twice, with swift, sharp slaps across his face, trying to knock some sense in him, but it never helped anything and she didn't know what to do here, with this almost old man raging like a bull through the house that was so quiet a moment ago.

Griet opens the door for Imogen, flustered and panicked, asking Griet, "What is wrong?"

"I don't know, he just came loose, and he too strong for me."

Imogen can hear her father, still smashing things already broken to smithereens, groaning and howling so loudly she wants to cover her ears but knows she has to find the strength in her somewhere to hold her father down and quieten him.

He was looking at his hands when she reached the top of the stairs, blood streaming from deep cuts on account of all that smashing – shards of glass, porcelain sharp at the edges. It looks as though he doesn't know what it was or how it got there, a vexed expression on his face. Imogen sees his hands need stitches, coaxes him into going to the hospital, his hands wrapped in towels and his face blank. Griet stays, insists that she will clean up the mess. Imogen tells her not to worry, to have a cup of tea rather.

"No, I make it right again, Miss Imogen."

Imogen explains to the doctor that her father is still in shock, that he needs to rest, needs some care. She convinces herself that, yes, he needs some psychiatric treatment, some kind of intervention that would contain him and make it less traumatic for him. The doctor stitches up William's hands, his face still blank and unmoved though it could have moved the earth back at home. The doctor agrees to transfer him to the psychiatric wing, makes notes on his clipboard.

William under white sheets, his skin blends into the stark, sterile surroundings, a drip in his arm, to calm him, the nurse said, to give his body a chance to rest up and heal. A ward for the depressed, the burnt out, eating disorders, botched suicides, nobody barking mad. Imogen holds her father's hand, stroking the fine hairs. Mother sits opposite, holding a small basket of dried fruit and biltong, a carton of fresh orange juice, tells him how much she hates hospitals. "Full of old and sick people, William, and now you have gone and landed up in the wing where they keep all the nuts!"

"Gran, really, he has had a hard day."

"He can't hear me, passed out cold he is, just making light, that is all, don't mean it, Imogen, trying to find the funny side."

"Don't think there is a funny side, Gran."

"No, I guess there isn't. Lord only knows what keeps us waking up everyday. You should get away too, there is the farm still, there will *always* be the farm, it was one of the clauses in the contract my mother and father signed.

Imogen doesn't know how Mother can launch herself into the beginnings of another story when William is lying in hospital too tired to care anymore.

"I saved myself for my wedding night, heaven alone knows why. Do I regret it now! But nevertheless I did, unlike your great grandmother, Hannah, who lost her virginity to a boy no one ever wanted either, barefoot and skipping stones across the river. Because finding a husband was proving to be difficult, Hannah thought she would throw caution to the wind and see what all the fuss was about in case she never got to find out. Behind a boulder, his trousers around his ankles, her skirts lifted, the veins in his neck straining and your great grandmother always told me that she had been very disappointed, seeing it as a dull foretelling of married life. But Stefan had surprised her; she was waiting for the opportune moment to sigh, but heared something far more resonant coming from the pit of her stomach. She always told me that I shouldn't make the same mistake she made, should wait for a man I could really love or imagine loving. You could say, Imogen, that it never worked out that way for me, but I will get to that. There must be a lesson in it."

Mother pours a glass of orange juice, takes a small, neat sip. "Juice never sits well with me, it gives me acid, dear. Would you like the rest of my glass?" Imogen shakes her head.

"Well, where were we? Yes, Hannah losing her virginity to the village idiot and finding happiness with another. After Father Wilson died, Adriana never quite came back to her old self, feeling the tiredness in her bones quicker than she used to. She still put me on her shoulders and told me stories about the sky and birds and the turning of the seasons and I grew up at her side rather than at my mother's side. Your great grandfather would take me for walks, a pipe sticking out from the corner of his mouth, but I was never really close to him, though he thought I was a miracle from heaven. The farms being so close together it was easy to take the walk to Adriana, to find her rocking on the porch or pulling carrots, talking to the sterile bull, easy to clamber up onto her lap grown warm and welcoming with age.

As I grew older there was all that usual talk about husbands and families and Adriana never said much to me about it, Mother and Father always kept their eyes open, and Adriana told them to leave me alone, that it will all happen as it should. Hannah wanted me to be happy, but forgot that love doesn't knock on your door and ask you, 'Where have you been all this long and lonely time?'

"I married the first man that showed a bit of interest in me, Imogen, can you believe that? After all that Hannah said about love, I just went in blind. Your grandfather, Edward Elliot, was a mean one alright." Imogen didn't remember much about him, as he dropped dead of a heart attack before her sixth birthday. She remembers that he smelt of mothballs mingled with aftershave.

"His brother, Bruce, not much better. In fact, he was probably worse. They worked as accountants at a firm, in the ever-expanding town we would go to once a fortnight to stock up. My best friend, Hester, had married Bruce a year earlier, shot him dead with his own rifle just after you were born, getting him back for all the miserable years, being dragged from room to room by her hair, being beaten senseless. Sober as a judge she was, aiming between his eyes and pulling the trigger when he came through the door with some animal over his shoulder. The courts were sympathetic for once, considering the extenuating circumstances, giving her a five-year suspended sentence, sessions with the state psychiatrist. It was probably Hannah's testimony that helped her get off, soaked with blood and sympathy it was, telling the courts how many times she had to clean Hester up and nurse her wounds and that that bastard Bruce had got what was coming to him. Hester's two sons meek as lambs lest she got that rifle out again, her only daughter up and leaving one day.

"Edward asked me to a dance on one of our town trips, held at the local hall with cheap punch on offer. I had imbibed too much, of course, and Edward started to look like the best thing there was to be found in a town like that, where nothing really happened. We were married four months later, bells ringing and Hannah crying, Adriana not fooled by his charming smile. Stefan shaking his hand, welcoming him to the family, clinking a glass and the tins tied to our car rattling down the road towards our honeymoon at the coast. I was finally going to see the ocean, Imogen. Can you imagine that? My heart was fit to burst, I tell you, and I guess that was the happiest day of my married life. The only one."

You have forgotten the day I was born, Mother, or do children always think it must be the happiest when often it isn't, depending where you are really.

"The ocean was all they said it was, I could hardly contain it, make sense of it even, how huge and intimidating and playful it was. We lived a while in town, Edward making my life smaller, preventing me from doing the things I used to do even though I couldn't remember what they were, telling me a wife's place was at home, even the sex was rotten, Imogen. I know it isn't an image you probably want but life is as it is, like an automaton he was, selfish and brutish. Even if I didn't feel like it, which was never, it didn't matter to him, telling me that it was another one of my wifely duties. That was the first time he hit me with a closed fist, when I refused him. I knew I had made a terrible mistake marrying him but figured there was no way out, that I had made a vow, though he rescinded on his all the time.

"My parents getting old and the farm too big and too much for them, Bruce making an offer they couldn't refuse. Buying up their farm, Adriana's too but he could do nothing with it while she was still alive, she underlined it in bold. Hannah and Stefan could stay on the farm and it would always be open to future generations. Bruce, tired of numbers and columns, dreamed of a game farm, the farm's the perfect size for something private, special guests and tourists wanting to mount another head on the wall, take home a piece of Africa. He would make a fortune.

"So it began, selling off the jersey cows, the implements, building another house on the land for himself and a heavily pregnant Hester for the second time, their two-year-old boy aiming a toy rifle at a field mouse. 'One day you will be using real guns, son.' Well, that is what I would imagine he would say, Imogen, something inane like that."

A nurse stout and friendly comes in to check on the drip drip of William's somnolence. Mother offered her some dried fruit from her Red Riding Hood basket. The nurse replies that it always gives her gas.

"Well, Imogen, I guess you can't please everybody," Mother says, opening the packet, biting into a shrivelled slice of peach.

"It took me a long time to fall pregnant. Well, Edward expecting something to happen the first time he lunged into me, only happening seven months later when I woke up nauseous for no reason, never thinking of pregnancy. Hannah telling me I must be expecting, then, and I should stock up on water biscuits. I can't tell you I was happy, Imogen, I thought that I could get out still, if it was just me. Now I had your mother to think about, and everyone was so happy, even Edward praying furiously for a son, laying off the punches for a while.

He was horribly disappointed that I gave birth to a daughter, seeing it as a grave failing on my part, not realizing that it was all his doing, carrying that Y chromosome. I had blow all to do with it. He reminded me often of that failing, and he worked at it again, determined that I bear him a son. But I think I lost the enthusiasm to fall pregnant again. Your mother was a beautiful baby, not even I could resist her, really, and Hannah loved her the moment she laid eyes on her. Adriana, nearing eighty, cradling your mother in her arms how she must have cradled me when I was born. Edward holing himself up in his study working on other people's financial misfortunes or sudden runs of luck.

"We moved to Cape Town after Adriana died, Edward taking up a transfer offer. Your mother had just turned five and I was even excited, maybe a move away from the harsh land would soften Edward, maybe it would be good for us, I thought. Of course, the death of Adriana shot a hole through everyone's heart. Hannah not emerging from her room for days, Stefan bringing her tea, and kissing her gently on her forehead, closing the door again, figuring that when her crying was done, she would get up again, just like Adriana had done when Father Wilson died.

"It was me who found her, Imogen. I had left your mother with Dorothy, our domestic worker back then, Sarah telling Dorothy stories, getting under her feet, Dorothy always so patient, unlike me.

"I had been meaning to see Adriana, I had been

so busy with your mother and I had to wait for some bruises to fade, take care that I didn't incite fresh ones. I took the walk I always did as a child, remembering how different it looked on my grandmother's shoulders, the cool river, the grasses brushing against my bare legs and how it used to tickle and make me laugh.

"She wasn't on the porch, nor in the fields picking vegetables for the table, wasn't in the house either, its rooms eerily silent without her. I never thought she could die, I had immortalized her in my head, even when I was an adult it seemed unlikely that Adriana would ever lie down and die.

"I found her sitting in a slant of sun in the old barn, her arms slack at her sides, a spade on the ground near her feet. She was planning to dig into something. Maybe she felt dizzy and decided to sit for a while, leaning against the leg of a wooden work bench. I shook her, Imogen, shook her for all I was worth but she didn't wake up, didn't move, didn't make a sound.

"I sat there for what must have been a long time, sharing that bit of sun with her, leaning against her shoulder, tears I never thought I had or owned pouring out of me, not wanting to know anything about a world that didn't have her in it. I could have died right along with her, but I had your mother to think about, defenseless and vulnerable, and the ever-darkening road of my family's future, knowing I had stepped on the wrong path. So I swallowed hard and got up, went to find Hannah to tell her her mother was dead.

"We buried her next to Father Wilson, knowing that she would have wanted to be there with him, Bruce hardly allowing for any respectful length of time to pass, started the plans he had for Adriana's land,

Hester pregnant for the third and last time, shedding tears over Adriana's grave.

"We moved not long after that, me carrying on in that world without her. Edward finding a pretty home in a swanky suburb replete with forests and mountains to look at when it was ugly inside. We would go up to the highveld once a year, my parents grey and arthritic, and still in love after all the passing time.

"I would send your mother up in the Easter holidays, thinking a change of scenery would be good for her, that the less time she had to spend around her father and my problems the better. She would come back saying she didn't like it and I wondered what was not to like, all that space and her grandparents, Aunt Hester, a motherly type, and not cold like me. I never got to know why she didn't like it. She never told me." Mother bites into a wrinkly prune.

"You know, I have never liked dried fruit much, always feel sorry for it, as though you are always biting into the idea of what it was. Could do with a cup of tea too, feel a little peaky inside."

Imogen smooths the covers around her father, plumping up the pillows, says she needs to go.

"Yes, I think I will be going too, spent enough time here, makes me twitchy, dear."

The house is spotless again, Griet having swept and vacuumed and wiped down the walls. She leaves the spare key on the chest of drawers, a fragrant vegetable curry on the stove. Imogen was fine till then. Something about the effort Griet had put into it sent Imogen's eyes streaming again. Yes, Imogen, it is always the details that get you when you least expect it.

She should go home, seeing that there is nothing to

do here and no one to watch over, but she can't find the energy and finds it comforting to be in her childhood home. It is familiar ground. Wonders if she could go out, do something normal, laugh a little, but she doesn't feel like bracing herself against the shadows, and those walks through lonely parking lots to her car and wondering who could be behind her? She can hear the muffled drone of Mrs Watson's television next door, she can picture her with her feet up, knitting, a blanket around her knees, watching the images with one eye, cursing the news, getting up later to make a cup of tea, rubbing that aching spot on her back, missing the smell of that pipe still.

21

IMOGEN WAKES UP to the absurd cheerfulness of a breakfast programme, still in her clothes, the faint glow of a light she never switched off. She puts the pot on for coffee, takes a cup for her father, forgets that he is lying in another bed.

The warmth of the coffee steams up her glasses and she thinks that the world and the scenery looks better that way, everything softened to an unidentifiable haze.

She answers the ringing bell: Griet at the gate ready to tackle whatever the day brings. Imogen wonders what time she had to get up to be here at this time, even the birds are reluctant to start singing at this hour.

Griet looks like a flower growing out of a crack in the pavement, climbing up against the backdrop of a featureless sky.

"You going to let the *Hotnot* in?" Griet smiles.

Imogen blushes, not sure if she heard right; she opens the gate, not really sure what Griet could do, seeing that her father isn't around to look after and clean up after.

"Always something to do, Miss Imogen. I could sort out the cupboards, finish up from yesterday."

"It isn't necessary, really, have some coffee with me, don't worry with the Miss either, just Imogen."

"*Ja*, okay." Griet takes a packet of Rothmans cigarettes from her housecoat pocket. "Can I smoke?"

Of course she can, Imogen, I have been dying for a cigarette all this time.

Griet lights up, exhales a straight line of smoke from her thin lips, and inquires about William's state of health, stirs two sugars into her coffee. My daughter does not knowing really, he was asleep when she left, didn't know when he would be well again.

"How could he be the same after that?"

How could any of us be, Imogen?

"It was a terrible thing, Miss Imogen, that happened, I am sorry about your mother."

"I need to see someone today, I am doing research – well, supposed to be doing research – on the gangs for the university I work for. I can give you a lift home if you want. Take the day off rather." Imogen is not sure if she works anymore, she is thinking of giving it all up, running into those undulating hills.

"*Ja,* the gangs make everyone afraid, can't do nothing without the gangs saying so. Who are you seeing, talking to?"

"Tannie Piep, do you know her?"

"Ha, everyone knows Tannie Piep, even if you don't, she make sure you do, tries to clean up the place, one woman on her own. Some think she is crazy, putting herself in danger like that, me I think she is brave. She tries to get more of us older women fighting against the gangs, but we are all too scared, 'cause it's all our families involved and against each other and family. Well, you know *mos,* can't speak against it, will get you killed if you do. How Tannie Piep has stayed alive, we don't know."

Imogen couldn't imagine anyone wanting to silence Tannie Piep, coming to look at the rooms she once lived in, the cookies on the plates, the spice jars neatly labelled and stacked. That swan on the television set, those innocent gestures against a world gone mad and would they think they had done good, that Tannie Piep had got them good.

Griet stubbs her cigarette out in the hand-painted ashtray I bought from some market, guinea fowls pecking at seeds. Imogen looks for her keys, rinses the cups in the sink. Out with Griet into the blue day. Griet walks up a different set of clanging stairs and waves goodbye to my daughter.

Tannie Piep is in good spirits, it is a sunny day and she has hung out her sheets, dusted, even got Esmeralda off to school. She thought this was a day to bolster the sails of the otherwise deflated women, incense them into taking action, to save the neighbourhood.

"We are planning a march, Imogen. A thousand candles burning over the sound of gunshots, but we will carry on marching and marching till the bloodshed stops and our children can come out to play again."

"My mother was murdered." Imogen just blurted it out, her eyes focused on a piece of lint on her slept-in trousers.

Tannie Piep failed to find the train of thought she was on, sighing heavily into her blouse, pink today with tiny blue flowers.

"She was raped too. I try not to be angry, I even try to understand but I don't know if I can, is there any use in understanding, what if you understand the wrong way?"

"Lovey, I am so sorry, so very sorry; the police catch anyone yet?"

"No, they haven't found anything, just the car that

was taken."

I can show you Imogen, take you to one of the men, I saw him running up the stairs, stopping to talk to Griet, she looked as if she was shouting at him, slapping the cap off his head, like a mother would. I know where he is, Imogen!

"*Ja*, the police good for nothing, hardly see them here, or they too busy taking bribes; these are sad things you are telling me here." Tannie Piep reaches into her bra, takes out a crumpled tissue, dabbing her eyes.

"My father is in hospital, suffered some nervous breakdown yesterday, the shock is too much for him, he's getting old." Shocks you when you are young too Imogen, I know you still don't know what to feel yet.

"I'll make you some tea, lovey, a sweet strong cup," says Tannie Piep, squeezing Imogen's hand. Getting up to set out plates and cups and saucers, neatly on her tray, setting out all the time and the loved she has lost.

I feel this string keeping me here losing its grip, its hold, my memory of sight blurring, my adapted movement starting to disobey me again. My hearing is fading and the world is moving further and further away from me. I don't remember the wind much anymore, nor arms thrown around me, forgetting that I danced once, forgetting the paths to places I used to go to, not caring much to find words anymore.

Imogen sits opposite one of her professors, tells him that she doesn't know when she will be back. She says she needs some time to think or think nothing at all. She pictures herself coming back, of course, older, locking herself in an office typing words nobody reads, and she would smell of lavender and drive her grandmother's bronze Mercedes. She would leave the tea cups in the sink because it was just her at home, you know. The professor wishes her well on her sabbatical, or not sabbatical, she didn't know which. She just wants to drive and put a great deal of distance between her and the memory of me.

She has my ashes with her. A travelling suitcase filled with only the essentials: a few books, a fat bank bag of pot, bought from a man she trusted, dreadlocks underneath an over-sized tea cozy. She didn't think William would mind about me in that cookie jar, letting me go was something Imogen wanted to do.

She had phoned our almost forgotten family at the farm, telling Hester, now almost blind and certainly hard of hearing that she was coming, to rest. They had sent their condolences in the form of a card and an arrangement of flowers for the funeral, but said, "Well, it's far and we won't be able to make it." Hester had sounded pleased Imogen was coming: "You didn't even reach my knee last time I saw you."

Mother said she would look in on William, watch over him and keep Imogen up-to-date. "Say 'hello' for me, dear. Send my love."

The long flat desolation of the Karoo, flocks of sheep huddled under a single tree, jagged mountains and everything parched with thirst, Imogen staring ahead, the road hypnotic, punctuated with welcoming mirages.

Where are you taking me Imogen? I don't want to go back there, it took so long to begin to forget! Further and further up, knots of civilization, knots of nothing, the bend in the road, the rusted tractor just as

I pictured it, the old house where Adriana used to live, the candles blown out.

Up a stony and potholed drive to a bigger house and Hester waves from the porch.

She squeezes Imogen's cheek, forgetting that she is a grown woman. "My, look at you, all grown up." Hester, who is basically a stranger to Imogen, doesn't quite know how to react, or what to say. But they are family one way or the other and that has to count for something, give them some common ground to walk on. "How have you been, you know with..."

"Okay. Dad isn't doing too well, thank you for letting me come."

"Pardon?" Hester holds her hand to her ear. "I am a little hard of hearing, you have to shout."

"I'm fine. We are all fine; thank you for having me."

"Always welcome, dear. You must be tired, would you like a sandwich? Was just about to make one myself, been lonely in this big old place since my boys got married. Dirk moved into old Hannah's house, John built another for himself, I got three grandchildren all grown up like you and only one of them stays at the farm. The rest scattered to the cities dreaming of big things, though no bigger dreams than the ones found here, I always thought. Been lonely for a long time, then. *Ag,* listen to me going on like this like an old woman when you have the world of worry in your eyes." Hester took out a thick white farm loaf of bread, pickles she had made herself, cold meats, a jar of wholegrain mustard. Imogen tried to picture her with a rifle in her hand blowing her husband away.

"My boys, they still come and see their old mother, they wouldn't hear the end of it if they didn't, fill me in on their days, taking tourists around on those hunting trips, close shaves with bad tempered buffaloes and rifles jamming sometimes. Never see my daughter anymore, I don't even know where she is, she took off one day and never came back. I think she ran off with that woman who worked at the local pet shop, she disappeared around the same time my daughter did. I would like to know, well, if she ended up happy. It is important isn't it?"

Imogen eats the sandwich out of politeness; she still isn't hungry and wishes that her appetite would return.

"I made a room ready for you, up in the attic, I thought you would like that, got a nice view of the mountains and at night you can hear the river just like it was the ocean right next to you."

"Thank you. You didn't need to go to any trouble."

"No trouble at all. Come, I'll show you where it is."

Hester leads the way up the stairs, her legs stiff and slow, her breathing laboured. Ascending past framed black and white photographs in perfectly straight lines. "See, I told you you would like it."

Imogen can't complain, a wooden bed covered in a quilt, plump white pillows, a tiny window opening onto the indigo hills beyond, miles of bush and thorny trees and small birds in almost every one of them, perched on the bleached white needles.

"Hannah, your great grandmother, made that quilt, almost made herself blind sewing it up, working at it every night, saying she wanted to give me something special. I miss her sometimes, the farm never the same without her really, nor without Adriana. Well, you'll be comfortable here, dear, take all the time you need. Freshen up if you want to."

"Thank you." Imogen feels exhausted, thinks she will lie down for a nap and listen out for the river.

I used to sleep in this room too, Uncle Bruce tucking me in. I always wanted to stay with Hannah, but they would bring me here sometimes. They always said Hester loved me so and I could play with my cousins, and wouldn't I find it boring with two old people?

I would kick up a fuss sometimes and refuse to move from my grandmother's arms. She never knew what came over me, only told me to stop having the fits and that Hester would have been hurt by my behaviour. So I went reluctantly, and wished that Hannah would come back to rescue me, wished that she would barge through the door at the right time, so that she would see. Imogen sleeps through the night. Hester came in to pull the quilt around her, setting another sandwich down on the table in case she woke up hungry.

Eating breakfast together, Hester says, "You hardly ate a thing. The air around here will make you strong again, dear."

She takes the road down to the old house, the cookie jar in her arms, the grasses leaning out into the road and brushing against her trousers. The old house still slanting and the fence still rusted, the gate hanging from a single hinge. The old slaughterhouse modernized now, horns nailed to its walls and pictures of proud tourists with their kills, meat drying on hooks.

Down through the gravel path pink and white with wild cosmos, the soft clearing and the now towering tree that cast needled light.

The grave stones mottled with lichen, crumbling in places.

Adriana next to Father Wilson, Hannah next to Stefan and, I guess, Mother will want to be here when her time comes.

Imogen takes the lid off and sets the jar down on the ground, taking out my ashes. Opens the bag.

She stalls for a while, just sits there on her haunches saying things I can't hear anymore, the world having grown silent in me.

She gets up and wipes her eyes with the back of her hand, scatters me from her hands, the wind picking some of me up, taking me elsewhere. Most of me settles over the stones of my mothers and over the men who knew how to let them be free.

Imogen walks with her back against the boarded windows, against the hills her eyes can't take in yet.

I can't tell you what it is like to disappear, can't tell you about possible light or choirs returned to me, or the ones I have missed coming to meet me. I can't tell you about the vast expanses of emptiness where nothing waits for me. Cannot tell you that my last thought looked like a circle.

**Previous winners of the
European Union Literary Award,
all available in Jacana paperback:**

2006/07
Coconut
Kopano Matlwa

2005/06
Bitches' Brew   *Ice in the Lungs*
Fred Khumalo   Gerald Kraak

2004/05
The Silent Minaret
Ishtiyaq Shukri

Rules for entry into the 2008/09
European Union Literary Award can be found
on the Jacana website: www.jacana.co.za